BRENT LIBRARIES

Please return/renew this item
by the last date shown.
Books may also be renewed by
phone or online.
Tel: 0333 370 4700
On-line www.brent.gov.uk/libraryservice

THE LOVE HYPOTHESIS

Laura Steven

First published in Great Britain in 2020
by Electric Monkey, an imprint of Egmont UK Limited
2 Minster Court, 10th floor, London EC3R 7BB

Text copyright © 2020 Laura Steven

The moral rights of the author have been asserted

ISBN 978 1 4052 9694 6

A CIP catalogue record for this title is available from the British Library

70491/001

Printed and bound in Great Britain by CPI Group

Typeset by Avon DataSet Ltd, Bidford on Avon, Warwickshire

Stay safe online. Any website addresses listed in this book are correct at the time
of going to print. However, Egmont is not responsible for content hosted by third
parties. Please be aware that online content can be subject to change and websites
can contain content that is unsuitable for children. We advise that all children are
supervised when using the internet.

Egmont takes its responsibility to the planet and its inhabitants very seriously.
We aim to use papers from well-managed forests run by responsible suppliers.

For Louis – because I love you more than
any hypothesis can explain

Allow me to explain the plethora of ways in which my love life is screwed. You know, scientifically.

According to the Matching Hypothesis, two people are more likely to form a successful relationship if they're equally desirable. This desirability can come in the form of wealth or fame, but it's usually determined by physical attractiveness. Which is to say: most folks fall in love – and stay in love – with other folks on the same level of hotness.

Back in the sixties, social scientists held a Computer Match Dance which, despite its cool name, was nowhere near as fun and futurey as it sounds. Basically, four judges rated a bunch of participants according to their hotness, and these participants were randomly paired up for the dance (except no man was paired with a taller woman, because god forbid their masculinity be challenged in any way!). During an intermission, participants were asked to assess their date, and the results showed that partners with similar levels of hotness expressed the most liking for each other. Shocker, I know.

The sixties may as well be Tudor England, but unfortunately this theory holds true in the internet dating age. One recent study measured the hotness of sixty men and sixty women, and their interactions were monitored. While people at least attempted to contact others who were significantly hotter than they were (probably because the variable of face-to-face rejection had been eliminated, as is the appeal of all online dating), it was ultimately found that the person was way more likely to reply if they were closer to the same level of hotness.

No, you haven't stumbled upon a social psychology journal by accident, like I did one heady night while researching Walster and Walster over a glass of 2003 Merlot.

All I'm saying is that if the Matching Hypothesis is anything to go by?

Yikes.

1

His name is Haruki, and he doesn't know I exist. I know, I know. It's a high-school cliché. But clichés are usually clichés because they're true. And this particular cliché — nerdy-comma-unpopular-girl-falls-for-hot-guy — is only ever a recipe for disaster.

Haruki bleeds charisma. You know the type. A jock who walks the halls surrounded by disciples like he's the second coming of Christ, or whatever. His family is basically royalty in my small town, since they own a multi-million dollar hotel chain that dominates most of the midwest. And it helps that Haruki is practically a supermodel, despite having the same basic haircut as every other attractive teenage boy in America. Plus we're in all the same AP science classes, and while he's hardly at the top of the pack, he is whip-smart.

So, to sum up: Haruki Ito? Way out of my league. Like, we're not even playing the same sport.

It should come as no surprise to you that I'm not the only

girl at Edgewood High who's madly in love with Haruki. And, as per the unrequited love trope, I'm utterly convinced I'm the only one who *gets* the real him. Despite, you know, him not knowing I actually exist.

(I cannot emphasize this last part enough. I could perform an elaborate macarena in front of his desk right now, and he'd stare straight ahead as though the light was simply bending around me. Maybe it is. I can never know for sure.)

Today we're in double AP Physics, which sounds like a cruel and unusual punishment to the normal high-schooler, but seeing as I'm not a normal high-schooler, this is my idea of utopia.

I adore science. Not so much biology, because it's all kinda messy and unreliable and oftentimes smelly. Or chemistry, because I still have scar tissue on my left hand following a bunsen burner incident a few years back. But physics? Physics is my dirty talk. It's clean and neat, and simple and complex, and it makes perfect sense to me. It's one of the few things that does. So, if you ever want to lure me into the boudoir, talk Newton to me.

Mrs Torres is delivering a lesson on the behavior of gas at room temperature, but since I've been pretty much fluent in thermodynamics – and most other aspects of classical mechanics – since I was thirteen, she's been giving me college-level modern physics papers to quietly work through during class, providing I a) complete all the regular homework too, and b) don't tell any of my classmates. So I'm doing some reading around antimatter and barely paying attention to the lesson when Haruki pipes up.

At the sound of his voice, something skips in my chest. (Upon reading this sentence, my very literal dad will almost definitely have me tested for arrhythmia.)

'But Mrs Torres,' Haruki says, interrupting her mid-flow. She nods for him to go on. 'Near absolute zero, the Maxwell-Boltzmann distribution fails to account for the observed behavior of the gas. So surely we should instead be using modern distributions, such as Fermi-Dirac or Bose-Einstein?'

I lay down my pencil with interest. Torres wipes her forehead with the back of her hand. The classroom is sweltering in freak late-September heat. 'That's correct, Haruki.'

He frowns and asks, in a way that entirely suggests he already knows the answer and just wants to make a point, 'So why aren't we using such distributions?'

She sighs, swatting away a buzzing fly. 'Because quantum physics is not taught as part of this state's high-school curriculum.'

'Why not?' Haruki persists, like a dog with a bone. A really, really sexy dog. Not that I'm weirdly into dogs, or anything. Anyway.

The other kids shift restlessly in their hard, plastic chairs, silently willing their classmate to drop it. Their impatience is almost palpable, but drop it he does not. Instead he adds, 'If we can handle it, why not teach it?'

Torres presses her lips together and sighs again. It's two in the afternoon, and only getting hotter. Ah, climate change. I don't blame her for getting irritable, although Haruki has a point – a point my dads have argued time after time with the school board.

But patiently as ever, she says, 'Because truly getting to grips with some of these concepts requires an incredibly advanced level of math. Research shows that your average seventeen-year-old is unlikely to achieve such a level.'

Haruki scoffs. 'So what, we dumb down the syllabus to suit the lowest common denominator?'

I agree with what he's saying, but he's being kind of an ass about it. It's not Torres' personal fault.

Torres leans back against her desk and pinches the bridge of her nose. She's wearing heeled pumps, a tight blouse and even tighter pencil skirt. I feel sweaty and uncomfortable just imagining wearing something like that. Right now I'm extremely grateful that our school's lax uniform policy allows for shorts and flip-flops. My toenails are basically a hate crime, but the open air setup is a life-saver.

Patiently, Torres answers, 'I'm sorry, Haruki, but that's just the way it is. So if we could bring our attention back to –'

'Well, it's clearly *not* the way it is,' Haruki snaps, laying down his pencil. 'Because Caro Murphy seems to be above learning classical mechanics. Unlike the rest of us.'

At the sound of my name, I freeze in my chair.

Well, kind of my name. It's Caro Kerber-Murphy. But whatever.

Everyone else in the class bar Haruki snaps around to stare at me, gauging my humiliation levels following the public call-out.

I mentally flail for an explanation as to how Haruki knows two-thirds of my name. The assumption I'd made regarding my light-bending skills has been blown out of the water.

A loaded silence follows. What am I meant to do in this situation? Pretend I didn't hear him? Defend myself? Defend Torres? Why is there no textbook on how to navigate mortifying confrontations such as these? Maybe there is. Maybe I could Amazon Prime it right here to this very classroom. Do they do next-second delivery yet? Surely they're working on it?

Since the R&D bods over at Amazon clearly give no shits about my predicament, I do what all introverted science nerds would do in this scenario: pretend there's no outside world and stare defiantly at the CERN experiment outlined on the page in front of me.

Through the roaring pulse in my ears, I vaguely hear

Torres say, 'See me after class, Mr Ito. We'll discuss it then.'

My heartbeat takes a good half hour to return to normal cardiovascular function. In that time, I obsessively analyze the events of the past few minutes.

Firstly, it transpires that Haruki Ito is in fact aware of my existence, which is a significant development in itself.

Secondly, it appears that said awareness is founded on disdain for the special treatment I receive. Which, you know, fair enough. I'd be similarly pissed.

But the lovesick puppy in me is now worried. What if aforementioned disdain overrides any and all romantic feelings in the past, present and future, and in all dimensions up to and including those we have not yet discovered?

When final bell rings, I quickly chuck pencils and erasers back into my leather pencil-case and sling my backpack over one shoulder, into the neat dent carved from years of textbook-hauling. Seriously, being a devoted lifelong nerd has permanently messed up my posture and overall anatomy. I am essentially Quasimodo, if Quasimodo were an expert in kinematics. Maybe he was. We just don't know.

Painfully aware of the fact that I have to pass Haruki's desk to reach the door, I tuck my head to my chest and practically tiptoe past him. Just as I'm crossing the front of his desk, he clears his throat. That annoying, crush-induced arrhythmia strikes up again, and I stop walking to look up at him. For a sweet millisecond, hope bubbles in my belly. Our eyes meet, and it's . . .

Exactly as devoid of interest as I'd expected. It's soon embarrassingly apparent that he wasn't clearing his throat to get my attention. He was just clearing his throat. Because mucus. And, like an idiot, I stopped walking and gazed hopefully up at him.

He shoots me a look as if to say, 'What on earth are you staring at, you insignificant gnat?' and carts himself off to talk to Torres.

I shuffle meekly away, downbeat and dejected. By the time I've made it to my best friend's locker, I'm pretty sure Eeyore has replaced the bald eagle as my official patronus.

'Hey, girl. What's up?' Keiko asks. Her sunflower-print skater dress and blue ombre hair are an assault on the eyes but, like, in a good way. She's plugged into purple headphones, some new indie band playing in her ears, so she barely hears my mumbled reply.

Haruki knows who I am. He just doesn't care.

2

Keiko walks me to chess club. School's basically deserted, but she knows I still don't like to talk about anything personal while wandering the hallways – seriously, do you *know* how high the chances are of being heard? – so she just takes my mind off the situation by talking about a gig she's playing at the weekend.

Her mom's finally given her the green light to perform in drinking establishments with her rock band, which has opened up a whole new world of venues for her. She's only seventeen, but she has the voice of an old soul. And she writes all of the band's songs. What I'm trying to say is that my best friend is way too cool to be hanging out with me.

'So I'm thinking we'll open the set with *Mess You Up*, because that never fails to get the crowd going,' she says, all wide eyes and animated hand gestures. Her new bangs keep dropping into her face, and she brushes them back impatiently. 'And then a couple more uptempo bangers – *The Power of*

Pretty, Upside Downside — before mellowing out into *Reason To Be*. What do you think? Or should we skip the slow tracks altogether? I know some crowds prefer . . .'

And just like that she's off on another tangent. It's how our friendship has operated for over a decade. She talks, I listen. Mostly. And I'm okay with it. Mostly.

We walk past Emily and Ethan, the Griffin twins, as they check the school play audition times on the noticeboard. They both look up adoringly at Keiko as she passes — then exchange daggers when they realize what the other is doing.

Keiko has this magnetic energy. It's not the fact she's a rock star, or the fact she's done some plus-size modeling, or her quirky fashion sense and killer hair. It's all of those things, and something else entirely. A spark you can't put your finger on.

Basically everyone in school is in love with my best friend, but she never affords them the luxury of falling in love back. She's a big fan of hookups and fuck buddies, but not so much actual dating. Between her and Gabriela, our beautiful Puerto Rican cheerleader pal with a long-term boyfriend who loves her, is it any wonder ya girl's got self-esteem issues? (I know. I can't really pull off saying 'ya girl'. It's a problem.)

Keiko leaves me at the door with a hug, all warmth and stale cigarettes and sweet perfume. 'Go kill some kings, or whatever.' She says this every single time I play chess.

She's one of those people who proudly does not engage with nerd culture. I've tried telling her that superhero comics and board games are totally mainstream now, and that rejecting them ultimately means *she's* the one who's out of touch with the zeitgeist, but that put her off even more. She's so edgy I can barely keep up with what does or does not constitute a Cool Thing.

I'm one of the last to arrive, and almost everyone is already set up in a pair by the time I abandon my backpack and scan the room for a partner. Lucy Cox and Everett Clark hold hands over their board, gazing lovingly into each other's eyes, talking about new set pieces they've been learning. Madison Spencer and Guadalupe Martinez kiss over their warring queens, completely oblivious to the room around them.

God. When did chess club get so horny?

In fairness to the Matching Hypothesis, both couples are approximately the same level of objective hotness and social status. And I can't fight the twinge of jealousy. In a completely pointless exercise in self-flagellation, I catch myself wondering what kind of couple Haruki and I would be. Over-the-top PDA? Fake-arguing while sparks fly? Nerding out over mutual interests?

Doesn't matter. The Matching Hypothesis actively forbids us from ever dating.

I'm not sure why the Matching Hypothesis plays on my mind so much, to be honest. I stumbled upon that first article at a time in my life where I felt totally and utterly unlovable – when Gabriela and Ryan first started dating, and Keiko was at the height of her experimentation stage. Maybe that's why I latched on to the theory like a barnacle to a speedboat. I liked having a reason – a concrete, scientific reason – to explain why I wasn't in the same place they were, no matter how much I wanted to be. It gave me something to blame beyond myself.

Sighing deeply, I force myself back into the present. When I see the only person left unmatched with a chess partner, I nearly turn and walk straight back out.

Mateo grins as he watches me scan the room, waiting for the moment I realize my fate. When I try and fail to disguise my horror, he saunters over with a cocky grin.

'Caro Kerber. Looks like it's you and me.' Seriously, what is it with people only knowing two-thirds of my name? He drags a chair back along the ground, its legs screeching against the linoleum. 'Pull up a pew. I don't bite.'

Mateo Gutierrez is one of the most opinionated *homo sapiens* on this earth. He's president of the debate team, and he's renowned for having no concrete stance on, well, anything. His actual genuine views are lucid, whether political, social or ethical, but what does not change is how passionately he's prepared to argue on any given subject, from any given side of the debate. It's quite impressive. You know, if you find contentious, belligerent jerks impressive. Which I do not. At all.

'Alright,' I grumble, resigned to spending at least the next fifteen minutes in his presence. He's one of Gabriela's childhood friends, so I attempt civility at all times. 'Do your worst. And it's Kerber-Murphy.'

We've clashed during chess club on many the occasion. He usually beats me, with his calculated precision and meticulously executed set moves, but there have been a few times he's knocked over his own king in frustration. I'm a hideously defensive player, and fortify my pieces in such a way that they're impossible to penetrate. It drives him up the wall. And to be honest, it drives me up the wall too. I wish I was confident enough to push for bold attacks and risky sacrifices, but I'm not. I play it safe, always.

This time, it only takes a few moves for Mateo to launch his verbal assault. 'Coward. Do you know how boring you are to play against? I would say it's like watching paint dry, but that's offensive to paint.' He launches an assault with a knight and a bishop, but I've arranged my frontline so there are no hanging pieces. He groans in frustration.

I find myself in a position I so often land in: everything is so neat and impenetrable that I don't want to move anything when my turn comes around. I reluctantly shuffle a pawn forward. Mateo's eyes light up, and he swoops into the gap I've been forced to create. His eyes smirk, even though that's technically not a thing. It's the only way to describe it. He's obviously delighted with himself.

Said grin soon vanishes when he realizes I've forked his bishop and his knight, which is unfortunately nowhere near as dirty as it sounds. Just means he's about to lose one of them.

'Damn,' he grumbles. 'Lucked your way into that one, didn't you?'

I maintain a neutral expression. 'Totally. Pure luck.'

It's a little cooler in this classroom, since it's north-facing and all, but I'm still feeling clammy and uncomfortable. There's almost definitely going to be a sweaty assprint on this seat when I stand up.

Apart from a whirring ceiling fan, the room is graveyard quiet, and ripe with the sound of concentration. Until Mateo pipes up again, since he basically has to be making some kind of noise at all times, and starts humming an annoying tune from a commercial I can't quite place. If he's trying to put me off, it's working. I can barely focus on the board, I'm so hot and bothered.

But then I see it: the intention behind his last couple of moves. He's visibly angry when I castle just in time to stop him from skewering my queen to my king.

What I want to say in response: 'I'll skewer your ass to your face, you pugnacious prick!'

What I actually say: 'Please be quiet, Mateo. Some of us are trying to concentrate.'

Look, I don't mean to sound like Hermione Granger every minute of the livelong day. It just happens.

We play for a while longer. I try to regroup and fortify my defenses, but his unrelenting attacks punish my piece count. It's not going great, but at least I don't have any brainspace left to think about Haruki and our awkward encounter.

After ten more minutes, I'm not surprised when he promotes a pawn and effortlessly checkmates me.

At this point Mateo could choose to be gracious in victory, but as it happens, that is not the path he takes. 'Suck it, Kerber! What's that now? Eleven games to three? Twelve? I lose track.' He whistles unnecessarily. 'You need to grow some lady balls. Launch an attack. Maybe take your queen out for a joyride every once in a while. Or, you know, keep making a dick of yourself. Your call.'

I swear to god, I'm going to shove a rook so far up his ass he'll be able to taste wood varnish on the back of his throat.

By the time I leave school at five-thirty, the temperature is vaguely less hellish, so my walk home is bearable at least. Despite the absurd amount of thunderflies in the air.

I live a couple miles from school, which I diligently cover on foot every single day on account of Dad #1's obsession with car accidents. If you ever need to know hard statistics on how many people are killed in crashes each year, he's your guy. As far as fetishes go it's pretty niche, but I'd rather his search history showed repeated hits on government data sites than on hardcore pornography. You take the wins where you can.

At least the route home is pleasant. My neighborhood is a nice one; my dads are both tenured academics, so we live in the more affluent area of town. However, when you're a chronic overthinker, walking four miles a day with just your own thoughts for company is a special kind of hell. And before you suggest podcasts or audiobooks, yes, I have tried them. Doesn't work. My cogitation is louder than any headphones can plausibly go. I experience the audial equivalent of reaching the end of a page, then realizing you've absorbed precisely nothing because you're so busy fixating on an embarrassing thing you said back in kindergarten.

Tonight is no exception. As I pass preppy spandex-clad joggers, Labradoodles in appalling Swarovski collars, and an implausible number of 4x4s, all I can do is replay the painful encounter with Haruki over and over again.

The public call-out. The subsequent loaded silence. The heat — oh god, the heat. Like my cheeks were being

17

flame-grilled and served as the steak portion of a surf 'n' turf.

As if that weren't bad enough, the ass-clenching moment when I stopped at the sound of his throat-clearing, and it became immediately, excruciatingly apparent that he was not clamoring for my attention.

And the look. The look he gave me – like I was nothing to him. Which I guess I am.

I take my time ambling home, in no rush to discuss what I learned at school today with my dads over dinner, like I do every night. Blame the heat, or the emotions, or the ABSURD QUANTITY OF THUNDERFLIES, but for whatever reason, my heels are dragging.

Argh. Why do I even care so much about Haruki's lack of interest? I'm used to the whole unrequited-love deal. It's not new to me. I should be better at handling it by now.

Because it's definitely a pattern. A pattern with no outliers, no anomalies, no exceptions. Just data point after data point after data point of rejection. No, not even rejection. Rejection would require the objects of my affection to notice me enough to reject me in the first place.

Actually, there is one almost-exception. Kevin Cartwright. He's a couple years older than me, and we had a string of hookups over the summer. It started with a drunken one-night stand at a house party – classy way to lose your V-plates, right? – and became a regular occurrence whenever he'd had so much as a sip of beer. But every time I texted him sober, he ghosted me. He only ever wanted to hook up when it was on his terms, and when his blood-alcohol level was past the legal limit.

One night – when he was super wasted – he told me he was still hung up on his ex, and that it wouldn't be fair to me to turn whatever we had going into something more. And even though I was starting to kind of like the guy, I tried my best to bury whatever feelings I had for him. I knew deep down it wasn't going anywhere.

Then he went away to college a few weeks back, at the same time as my older brother, and I haven't heard a peep since. Guess I was just a way to kill time, when the lights were low and the beer goggles were firmly in place.

I sigh, inhaling warm summer air. The streets are quiet, even by my sleepy town's standards. Nearby, an elderly man is cutting the grass with his shirt off. A grey-haired woman watches lovingly from the window. And, to be fair to the Matching Hypothesis, they are precisely the same level of hotness. Figures.

Pulling my phone out of my back pocket, I press the home button. My lock screen lights up: nada. No messages, no missed calls. Keiko will be rehearsing for tonight's gig, and Gabriela will be tutoring after-school Spanish. She speaks, like, seven languages, has a makeup Insta with a gazillion followers, and bakes the best banana bread in the literal world.

Then she'll be hanging out with her boyfriend, Ryan. They've been together since freshman year and are basically the same entity at this point. In fact, I'm not entirely sure she hasn't absorbed his personality via osmosis. She had some actual points to make about the NFL draft the other day. Still, they're pretty cute. He's always picking up egg and cheese bagels for her breakfast, holding up her ring light so she can take the perfect selfies, making her study playlists on Spotify.

When I think of being with Haruki, that's what I imagine. Not huge, grand gestures of rapturous romance. Not even necessarily the physical aspects of having a boyfriend. Just small, everyday kindnesses that let you know you're loved.

For whatever dumb reason, I unlock my phone and open up the message chain between me and Kevin. It's . . . confronting. The last three messages were all sent by me: a stack of shameless blue bubbles.

Hey, how are you? Are you going to Steph's party this weekend? Hope to see you there. *beer emoji*

Kevin! Fancy a drink tomorrow night? My dads are out of town. And there's red wine in the refrigerator. (I know. They're criminals. Room temperature or bust.)

Hey! Just a quick message to say I hope your big move to Penn State goes well. Hit me up when you're next home and we can catch up.

My skin crawls, reading them back. But they're not that awful, are they? I obsessed so hard over striking the right balance between casual and flirty. Between upbeat and sarcastic. Between perfect and, well, perfect. And it still wasn't enough to get his attention.

I can't help but feel, like I do 201,674 times a day, that it's all because of the way I look. The blank stares, the ghosted messages, the everlasting feeling of irrelevance. It has to be. Because I'm smart, I'm interesting, I'm funny (when I have the guts to actually crack jokes within earshot of other human beings). I'm a nice fucking person. And yet no guy has any interest. Why?

I'm about to shove my phone away when, as it always does, temptation strikes. What if this is the one time Kevin will reply? What if he's drunk at a daytime frat party, and I send a message at the perfect moment, and he actually responds? It would soothe my self-hatred, if only for a moment. And hey, if he ignores me – what's new? It can't suck any more than it already does.

So I do it. I fire off a quick, breezy text, watch as the 'delivered' sign appears, and bury the phone back into my pocket. Maybe if I don't look for a while, there will magically be a message waiting for me later tonight.

My pretty, faux-Edwardian house is detached and modestly sized. Vati – Dad #2 – is out front gardening, and as I'm walking up the driveway I almost don't see him. He's about two inches from the soil, hacking away manically at the border with a pair of secateurs. He's a godawful gardener. Like, imagine you gave a donkey a pair of scissors and told it to go to town on your flowerbeds. That's how our garden looks.

But Vati loves it, so Dad just lets him crack on and do his thing. That is love, right there. And not that I've ever, you know . . . rated the hotness of my fathers, or anything, but they are pretty similar levels of good-looking and socially desirable. The Matching Hypothesis never fails.

'*Bärchen*!' he calls, dropping his tools and kneeling back on his haunches. Vati – Dr Felix Kerber – is Austrian. He's always called me *Bärchen*, ever since I was teeny. Little bear. It still warms my heart.

'Hey, Vati,' I say, stopping just short of the front door. 'How goes the gardening? *Zu heiß, nein?*' That's about as far as my German goes. Gabriela is the language goddess of our friendship tripod, and is completely fluent. Vati always loves when she visits.

'*Ja*, this heat is ridiculous,' Vati replies. 'And I'm making a real mess of this. I never did know what to do with bushes.'

And then he *guffaws*. Actually guffaws. At his own disgusting joke.

I mime gagging, and shout back, 'Is Dad inside? I would like some sensible conversation, for once in my life.'

Vati is too busy guffawing to respond.

Our dog Sirius – a one-eyed cockapoo – greets me at the door with a half-hearted tail wag. He is very old and very lazy, and his depth perception is very bad on account of the one-eye situation. Also, his face smells like a rotting corpse. Apart from that, I love him very much. Unfortunately, Sirius loves nothing but barbecue ribs.

I find Dad washing potatoes in the kitchen sink. Dumping my backpack on the counter, I immediately raid the fridge, as I do every night. And, as he does every night, Dad says in his dulcet Bostonian tones, 'You will ruin your dinner.'

He's the sensible one, Dad. While goofy Vati plays the clown, cracking inappropriate jokes and generally throwing caution to the wind, Dad is more subdued. As a world-leading expert in experimental hepatology, Dr Michael Murphy is not interested in your scatological humour. He is painfully smart, painfully literal, and affectionate in his own special way.

'Dad, there's every chance that the Higgs Boson being made over at the Large Hadron Collider are becoming unstable *at this very second*,' I say dramatically, while peeling a string cheese into my palm. 'By the time I've finished this sentence, one could have triggered a catastrophic vacuum decay, causing space and time, *as we know it*, to collapse.' Triumphantly, I cram several pieces of stringy deliciousness into my mouth. 'In which case, dinner will be ruined regardless.'

'Very good,' Dad grumbles. 'But since you have finished your sentence – and your snack – without a black hole in sight, you can close that fridge door, grab a vegetable peeler, and tell me about your day.'

3

Thanks to a potent dinner-table combination of intelligent conversation and creamy mashed potatoes, I manage to avoid checking my phone for a good couple of hours.

As I traipse upstairs, belly full of schnitzel, I'm almost dizzy with the anticipation of pulling my phone out and seeing Kevin's name light up my screen. Or Haruki's. Or anyone's, for that matter.

It's been two hours. I'll probably have several messages in my group chat with Keiko and Gabriela, comprising pre-show selfies like we always get from Keiko, and witty comments from Gabriela about the spoilt rich kids she tutors. Possibly even a missed FaceTime call, if Gabriela's particularly mad. Perhaps Leo, my brother, has tagged me in a nerdy meme only he and I would find funny. Maybe Haruki has reached out via Instagram to apologize for dropping me in the shit this afternoon. And surely Kevin will have replied by now, right? It's been two hours. Two hours!

For no real reason, I make a slight ceremony of the phone-checking. I get into comfy sweats and an oversized T-shirt, throw my hair up into a messy pony, switch on a couple lamps and my fairy lights, and curl up cross-legged on my bed. Dad must've put fresh bedding on this afternoon, because the plain white duvet cover with tiny pink flowers smells of lavender and camomile. That's when you can tell Dad is getting bored on sabbatical. He does all the laundry imaginable, instead of finishing the book proposal he's supposed to be working on.

When I'm finally ready, I press the home button on my phone.

Nothing.

Just the time – 9:01pm – and my background photo. Keiko and Gabriela's shiny faces smile back at me. We took that picture after Keiko's first ever gig, when we were all sweaty and high on adrenaline and good music. I'm sandwiched between the two of them, and you can barely see my face through Keiko's blue hair.

No texts. No calls. No notifications. Nada.

I shouldn't care. I know I have people around me who love me. Keiko and Gabriela, and my dads, even my big brother, although he's usually far too busy studying to pay me any attention. I know they care. It's just . . .

Technology today makes it so easy to constantly communicate with your loved ones. So when they *don't* communicate, when they all ignore you at once, it's the worst feeling. They *could* get in touch with you. They just don't.

I forever feel like everyone else gets more messages, more calls, more notifications than me. Everyone around me is forever looking down at their screen, laughing at something funny in their family group chat, swooning over a selfie from their crush, sighing as they faux-complain about how many notifications they have to read. And I just sit there, pretending to be doing the same, when really the only people who would ever message me are in the very same room.

It's pathetic, and I hate myself for caring. But I do. I just want a guy to text me and let me know he's thinking about me, to ask me how my day was, to send funny pictures to cheer me up when I'm down. It seems like everyone has that but me.

So, I do what I do almost every night when I'm down about my love life, or lack thereof. I whizz through my homework, take a long, hot shower, wait 'til my dads are both asleep – they usually hit the hay early – then sneak down to the refrigerator to retrieve half a glass of red wine. A full glass and they'd notice, but half usually slips under the radar, providing I remember to wash the glass and put it away again after I've finished.

Then I tiptoe back upstairs, lock my bedroom door, and engage in my dirty little secret: trashy rom-coms from the early noughties. Movies from before social media, before selfies, before the constant need for validation, before memes and Facebook politics. Just shamelessly cheesy romance and all the happy endings a girl could want.

My dads would murder me if they found me watching this crap. *It'll rot your brain cells*, they'd say. *Try this NASA documentary instead. Or if you have to watch a movie, at least start with Guillermo del Toro*.

But hey. You can't help what you love. And what I love is curling up in my empty bed with half a glass of red wine and watching cheesy rom-coms with the volume turned down low.

Ugly nerd on the outside, lonely middle-aged spinster on the inside. Form an orderly queue, fellas.

Tonight's pick is *Just Friends*, because I have a massive soft spot for Ryan Reynolds, like almost everyone with retinas. It's basically an in-depth study of the Matching Hypothesis. Ryan Reynolds' character doesn't get the classically hot girl until he changes everything about his physical appearance to match her level of attractiveness. Standard.

I've seen the film a couple times before, so I scroll aimlessly through my phone as I watch. Because I'm clearly a fan of torturing myself, I open up the conversation with Kevin — if you can even call a one-sided deluge of messages a conversation — and stare at my unanswered text.

Hey! You settling in okay? Hope you've managed to find a gaming buddy to replace Bryan.

And so begins the cringing.

Why did I have to go and make it so personal? I mean, he only told me about how much he was going to miss his gaming buddy because he was drunk. I'm pretty sure he did *not* want to be reminded of that. And here I go, dropping it into conversation like some kind of needy stalker. Does he think I'm a psycho for even remembering that? I bet he barely remembers what colour my eyes are, let alone the names of my best friends.

Hastily, just so I don't have to look at it any more, I delete the message, wishing this very act would remove it from his phone too.

I sigh, shove my phone under my duvet and lean back against the stack of pillows I've propped against my headboard. The TV and my fairy lights flicker in the darkness. The window is cranked all the way open, and the street outside is moonlit and peaceful, save for a few crickets chirping in the trees. The smell of warm sidewalks and cut grass drifts into my bedroom on the breeze. I take a sip of heady red wine, enjoying the rich, fruity flavour and faint buzz of alcohol. I feel young and old all at once.

Speaking of old, this time next year I'll be at college, if all goes according to plan. My first choice is MIT. Both my dads are alumni – that's where they first met – and Leo is there now, studying Chemical Engineering. It's a Kerber-Murphy family thing. And in twelve short months, I could be there too, studying Astrophysics at one of the best institutes in the world. I spent the whole of the tour visit I took this summer with goosebumps running up and down my arms.

That reminds me. Mrs Torres told me earlier in the week that she'd read over my personal essay and provide notes. I honestly don't know what I'd do without that woman. She's writing my letter of recommendation, too, and I have every faith she's going to knock it out the park.

I pull my phone out from its nook in the bedsheets and refresh my email to see if she's gotten back to me yet. Nope, nothing. Not even a single email. Seriously, am I some kind of leper? I text my group chat with Keiko and Gabriela just to make sure. It doesn't even deliver to Keiko, and even though Gabriela reads, she doesn't reply. She always does this – she's usually too busy hanging out with Ryan to answer.

Muscle memory leads me to perform my cursory evening perusal of Haruki's social-media accounts. He's the kind of guy who's way too cool for Instagram. He's popular without even trying. So as usual, he's uploaded precisely nothing today. His last post was a shot of Lake Michigan from the penthouse of his family's flagship hotel, where he spent most of his summer working as a kayak instructor. A few posts earlier is a picture of him helping a tiny kindergartner to buckle his life jacket.

Something twinges in my chest. I wish I was the kind of person Haruki Ito could fall for. I wish he would look at me the same way I look at him.

I shift in my duvet burrito, suddenly restless and antsy. I want to *do* something about this. About this perennial feeling of being unwanted. Undesirable.

Maybe science has the answer. Science can answer almost all of the important questions in the universe. So why not this? We've been studying love and attraction for centuries. We know that lust is governed by both estrogen and testosterone, and that attraction is driven by adrenaline, dopamine, and serotonin. Long-term attachment is governed by a different set of hormones and brain chemicals: oxytocin and vasopressin, which encourage bonding. Each of these chemicals works in a specific part of the brain to influence lust, attraction and attachment.

Surely, throughout hundreds of years of studying these things, someone has found a way to manipulate them? I mean, come on. Imagine possessing a wealth of knowledge in this field. That dark part of your mind would totally be tempted to manipulate that information to your advantage, no? To find a drug or hack to get other people to fall in love with you. Hedonistic renaissance dudes weren't exactly known for their moral compasses.

I pull up a new browser window on my phone and start researching whether anyone has ever attempted to manufacture these hormones and brain chemicals. However, all I find on Google are dating sites filled with hokey pseudo-science, and so-called 'love doctors' promising to transform the lives of even the most hideous *homo sapiens*. A cursory glance at some more academic sources pulls up social anthropology journals and neuropsychology papers which explore the theories behind love and attraction, but there's nothing to suggest they've attempted to put these findings into practice.

I'm about to give up and focus on Anna Faris singing 'Forgivenesssss' on my TV screen when an abstract catches my eye.

Scientists have discovered the key to attraction lies in a new type of pheromone which has recently been identified in the Brazilian Honey Beetle. The researchers behind the study, all three of whom are doctoral candidates at the University of São Paulo, believe that extracting this chemical and distilling it into pill form ...

The rest of the abstract is hidden behind a paywall. I run a search on the paper's author – Professor Pablo Sousa – and the university website comes up with several hits, all relating to his research on the Brazilian Honey Beetle. He's won several prizes for his work, and is now celebrating ANVISA approval of a drug prototype based on his findings. From what I can gather, ANVISA is the Brazilian equivalent of the FDA.

I'm desperate to read the entirety of the paper, and notice a small login portal beside the paywall, which grants access to those with an existing university ID. A dropdown menu shows they accept IDs from most major institutions, and I notice Vati's college on the list.

Inspiration strikes. Vati's desktop computer sits downstairs in sleep mode, with no password protection whatsoever. If his email account is open, I could simply request a password reminder, open and delete the email before he sees it, and use the deets to access this paper. I'm a genius.

As I pass their bedroom, Dad's earthquake snores rumble through the closed door. I stifle a laugh. He's such a quiet, restrained man, and yet his sleep apnea turns him into some kind of meteorological emergency. Between enormous snores, I can hear Vati muttering, '*Verdammt noch mal*, Michael!', which loosely translates as 'For fuck's sake.' He says something else along the lines of removing his throat with a machete, but like I say, my German is not great.

Leapfrogging over Sirius as he lies snoozing at the bottom of the stairs, I make it to the computer in the dining room and load it up. While I'm waiting for it to whir into life, I look at the photos taped to the bottom of the monitor with literal duct tape, because Pinterest-worthy our house is not. There's the four of us at the Rube Goldberg machine at the Museum of Science Boston; the four of us watching rat basketball at Discovery Place; the four of us playing mini golf at the Science Museum of Minnesota. In every single picture, Leo and I are concentrating intently, and Vati is pranking Dad – pulling pants down, drawing rat whiskers on him in Sharpie, using golf clubs to perform wedgies, etc.

As I open up Vati's email account, I can't help but grin. My dads are like my best friends, and my childhood has been so great. It's a bittersweet feeling, knowing it'll be over soon. There's something hollow beneath the bittersweetness, too, but I can't quite place it.

'*Bärchen?*'

Swiveling around, I see Vati standing in the doorway, fuzzy chest hair poking through the top of his bathrobe.

I leap back from the computer, as though I've been caught performing some kind of diamond heist. 'Vati. I was just, erm . . .'

'Hacking my emails.' He says this in a jokey way, i.e. the way he says everything ever.

'I thought you were asleep,' I say, as though this is a valid legal defense.

'*Nein, nein.* Dad *eins*, he sleeps like a woodchuck. Me? Well, what is the opposite of a woodchuck?'

I have no idea what a woodchuck is, nor how one might sleep, so I decide not to push the matter.

'What are you really doing, *Bärchen?*' he asks gently, perching on the edge of the oak dining table. He looks very tired, but also jolly, which shouldn't be possible.

I decide the truth isn't exactly incriminating, so I say, 'I need your institution login to access a research paper.'

'Ah, *wunderbar!*' he exclaims. 'Which paper?'

Chewing my bottom lip, I admit, 'It's about the laws of attraction.'

Vati's features soften. 'You like someone, *ja*? And you want to seduce them?'

'Please never say "seduce" again.'

'*Bärchen*, you don't need any papers to make a boy like you. You are the best person in the world, so. You can take poison on that.'

'Pardon?'

'Ah, maybe that is a German idiom.' Vati frowns and strokes his stubbled jaw. 'I think you say, "You can bet your life on that"?'

I chuckle. 'That makes more sense.'

He stands up and ruffles my hair, which is brave, considering it hasn't been washed in days. 'My password is *Bärchen*, followed by your birthday. Lower case, no umlaut. Because the university is racist, of course.'

'Of course.' I grin and hug him round the waist. 'Thanks, Vati.'

'No problem.' He kisses my forehead. 'As thanks, you can visit me in prison after I have removed your father's throat with a machete.'

Maybe my German isn't as bad as I thought.

A few minutes later, I'm back in bed with the full paper loaded on my laptop. My eyes skim down the five paragraphs over and over, trying to make sense of what I'm reading.

According to Sousa and other leading scientists in this field of study, the Brazilian Honey Beetle – particularly the female of the species – secretes absurdly high concentrations of an incredibly sophisticated sex pheromone, and researchers have now discovered a way to distill these chemicals into pill form, which are supposedly safe for human consumption.

When tested on rats, and later monkeys, the pills artificially increased an organism's ability to attract a mate tenfold. More relevantly, the report goes on to detail the clinical trials conducted with actual human participants, and while the results were not as potent as they were in rats and monkeys, the pills were found to quadruple the participants' ability to attract a sexual partner.

It sounds ludicrous. But for some reason, I sit up a little straighter. Because despite my intense cynicism, something about the idea captures my attention. And I'm no idiot when it comes to science. Okay, so pheromones are hardly my field of expertize, but the study and subsequent clinical trials at least sound plausible.

I spend the rest of the movie only half paying attention. Meticulously reading through each and every one of Sousa's articles, I familiarize myself with the subject as best I can. It sounds pretty interesting. And the best part? There's a link to buy the pills directly from the researchers. They're running a special trial price of $99 for your first month's supply – plus an eye-watering shipping charge to the US.

Despite my natural stance as an unfaltering cynic, I find myself genuinely considering it. Maybe I'm just feeling especially vulnerable after a day of rejection and loneliness, but the idea that there could be an easy fix out there is beyond tempting.

I imagine how good it would feel to walk into my next AP Physics class and have Haruki gaze at me with newfound attraction. I imagine walking the hallways and no longer feeling invisible. I imagine the confidence and self-worth I would feel, and the thought is so powerful that it almost knocks the wind out of me.

I imagine Haruki finally reciprocating my feelings. Bringing me bagels, making me playlists, sharing my hobbies and interests.

Shivering, I pull myself back to reality. It's a lot of money, and there's no guarantees the drugs will actually work. Besides, I'm supposed to be saving for college. MIT doesn't offer merit-based scholarships, because everyone who applies is a veritable genius, and I don't qualify for needs-based financial aid because my dads are tenured academics. They can help a little with tuition fees, but I still need to have a cushion under me to cover rent and food and all those other inconvenient human necessities. And since the comic-book store which used to employ me closed down, I've been out of work and struggling to find a new gig.

And yet . . . I can't get that image of myself out of my head. Chin tilted up, shoulders pushed back, walking with pride and self-assurance. Like Keiko does. The way she carries herself is something I've always admired. It's like she knows she's beautiful and deserving; like she knows she's worth something. I want that for myself. I want that so badly it churns in my chest, a sinkhole forming in my ribcage.

It's how I feel around my dads, I realize with a pang. Loved and wanted and respected. They make me feel funny, smart, beautiful. Special. Like nobody in the world could interest or inspire them more than me.

That's it. That's the way I want to feel all the time, no matter where I am or who I'm with. Because it's the greatest feeling in the entire world.

Suddenly I identify the strange hollowness I experienced when I looked at the pictures on Vati's computer. This time next year, I'll be living hundreds of miles away from my dads. What if I never get to feel that special again? What if I go through my college career – and the rest of my life – feeling the same way I do when Haruki Ito looks at me with nothing but apathy? The thought sends a lance of sadness through my heart.

Before I can talk myself out of it, I reach under my bed for my purse and pull out my debit card. A potentially imbecilic use of my birthday cheques, but the red-wine buzz has taken the edge off my inhibitions.

The Matching Hypothesis has been proven countless times. But what if this is the antidote?

4

The house is dank. The walls are dark. I've been here before.

The ceiling shifts and warps, and I know I am alone. I am small, and so terribly, terribly alone. My body tries to sweat, tries to cry, but there's nothing left inside. I am a husk, and the end is near. The walls bleed darkness, and the darkness bleeds fear.

Somewhere, a door opens.

I jolt awake, my snoozed alarm blaring into the sun-dappled room. Heart thudding, I turn it off and throw the tangled duvet off my sweaty legs.

I fucking hate that dream.

Every single morning, without fail. In that half-sleep, half-wake state of lucid cloudiness, the exact same dream. I push my fingers into my eyes until they turn into kaleidoscopes, forcing out the mental image of that damn room.

I was adopted by my dads when I was tiny, and I think these dreams are memories of my past life – of which I recall almost nothing. I have no *reason* to. Whoever my birth mother was, she's not around anymore. And my dads are. So why does my subconscious torture me? Why does it force me back into that room day after day after day?

For as long as I can remember, I've had these dreams, or flashbacks, or whatever the hell they are, while I'm dozing. And I still don't have the self-control to stop snoozing my alarm. Figures.

I pad downstairs in my Buckbeak slippers. Dad, who is much more well-rested than Vati and thus less likely to replace the sugar with arsenic, lays out the usual breakfast buffet. This sounds impressive, but really it's just a bunch of half-eaten boxes of cereal arranged by sugar content. As usual, I reach for the higher end of the spectrum, while Dad chows down on some sort of bran-based atrocity, washed down with tap water. Vati isn't into breakfast, so he pours himself a giant coffee and slumps into the third chair. For all his japes and hijinks, he is not a morning person.

'What are you guys doing today?' I ask, crunching into a brimming bowl of Lucky Charms. I chuck one to Sirius under the table, but he just stares at it like it's a hand grenade.

Dad finishes his mouthful of bran before responding plainly, 'I plan to visit the police station, on account of the fact we have been burgled.'

Vati and I both gape at him. 'What?'

41

'It is the most likely explanation.'

I look at Dad in bewilderment. 'Explanation for what?'

'The missing object.' His face betrays no emotion or affectation. He is impossible to read, even when you've lived with him as long as I have. You'd have more luck trying to psychoanalyze a park bench.

Vati drains his coffee mug and immediately pours another. 'What's missing?'

'Well, Felix, during my bi-weekly kitchen stock-take this morning, I discovered a discrepancy in the quantity of wine glasses in the bar cabinet. Wine glasses are sold in boxes of four or six, to reflect the nonsensical societal preference for even numbers, and yet our cabinet currently contains a mere five glasses. Having checked the trash to ensure none had been smashed or discarded, I deduced that one had been stolen in the night. Would you like to accompany me to the police station?'

Shit! The wine glass! I was so caught up in my covert pill-purchasing operation that I forgot to return the glass to the cabinet. It's still on my bedside, burgundy dregs turning to syrup in the bottom. I shoot Vati a panicked look, and he immediately understands what's happened.

Unfortunately, so does Dad.

'I see.' Dad lays down his spoon and folds his arms. This is much more serious than it sounds, because there's still bran cereal floating in the milk. Dad is not one to compromise the structural integrity of his breakfast by leaving it to swim in half-and-half. 'And how long have you suffered from alcoholism, Caro?'

I splutter, trying to compose myself. 'I'm not an alcoholic! I just had half a glass of red wine last night, that's all. Eighteen is the legal drinking age in Europe.'

'You're seventeen. And this is South Carolina.'

I try to fight the urge to roll my eyes. 'I'm not an alcoholic.'

'Why did you want a glass of wine?'

I shrug, pushing Lucky Charms around my bowl with my spoon. 'I dunno. I'd had a crappy day, alright?'

Dad nods knowingly. 'Classic sign of addiction.'

Bless his soul, Vati breaks the tension with a bark of laughter. 'Lay off her, Michael. It was one *kleine* glass of wine. No big deal. You're not going to do it again, are you Caro?'

'No.' I suspect this might be a lie, but still.

'And you're going to return the wine glass to the cabinet in immaculate condition, right?'

'Yep. *Ja.*'

'So, there's no problem, is there?' Vati smiles, even though it looks to be causing him great physical pain. 'You don't have to attend the police station today, Michael.'

Dad rises from the table, pours his ruined cereal into the sink, and starts toward the door. 'Perhaps I shall research the best juvenile rehabilitation programmes instead.'

I look at Vati, and we both press our lips together to keep from laughing. I polish off my cereal before the hilarity can escape. 'Okay, I gotta get to school.'

'Good luck with your seduction today.' He winks in a horrifying sort of manner.

As a furious blush spreads across my cheeks, I roll my eyes again. 'You're the worst.'

'*Danke*,' he says earnestly, bowing like some kind of royal thespian.

After the last class of the day, I meet Gabriela at Keiko's locker and we catch up about our days, since we all take such different classes. Keiko does most of the talking, as per, about how her art teacher is a pervert and her drama teacher is the single best human being on this earth.

Slamming her locker shut and popping a stick of gum into her mouth, Keiko says, 'What shall we do this weekend? My parents and dweeb sister are out of town and I don't have any gigs, so it's on y'all to entertain me.'

I accept a stick of gum and start chattering like a chimp. 'Oooh, there's this touring exhibit in town that I'm *dying* to go to. It's basically a bunch of artifacts from Pompeii, and there's a CGI simulation of the volcanic eruption at the end.'

'Spoilers,' says Keiko, affronted.

I gape at her. 'You didn't know Pompeii was wiped out by a volcano?'

'I thought it was just a catchy Bastille song.'

Honestly. How are we friends.

Shaking off my astonishment, I say, 'So are you in?'

Keiko looks like I might have suggested waterboarding each other in the creek. 'Museums are for the very old and the very tragic, and we are neither of those things. Gabs? Any ideas?'

Gabriela shrugs. She looks a little distant and jaded, and her winged eyeliner is smudged, which is pretty unusual for her. 'I think me and Ryan were just going to hang out at home. Watch some YouTube, eat some snacks. I dunno. I'm super tired lately.'

'Okay, grandma.' Keiko rolls her eyes. 'You are one hundred years old, and I'm overruling you both. Let's go see that new movie about the rock star who falls in love with her manager. It's basically the exact fantasy I get myself off to, so I can't promise not to start dry-humping the popcorn bucket.'

I snort-laugh in a very elegant manner. 'You are horrific.'

Keiko tuts and wags her finger in my face. 'That's slut-shaming and you're better than that. And also homophobic. Is lesbian sex so abhorrent to you?' I blush, and Keiko cackles at my panicked expression. 'Anyway, I gotta scoot,' she says. 'Detention again. Ah, the life of a misunderstood rebel.'

'Try not to dry-hump any desks,' I call after her as she sashays down the hallway in her skull-print dress. Gabriela, who hates sex-based banter, squirms beside me.

As she's about to turn the corner, Keiko presses herself against a wall of lockers and makes an elaborate groan of ecstasy. 'No promises. Toodles!'

Once she's shaken off the unspeakable horror of the last few seconds, Gabriela mumbles, 'I'll go with you to the Vesuvius exhibit, if you want.'

We start walking to the school gates. I grin gratefully. 'Thanks.'

Gabriela smiles, but it doesn't reach her eyes. 'Let's just . . . not tell Keiko, okay? That we're hanging out without her.'

This makes me feel a little weird – Keiko has been my ride-or-die since kindergarten – but I get Gabriela's point. Keiko only does what Keiko wants to do, but still gets upset when people do things without her. 'Agreed. Everything okay with you? You mentioned being tired a lot.'

Gabriela stares at her black Birkenstocks as we walk. Her nails are painted paprika red, and she wears a turquoise toe-ring. 'Yeah, I guess. I don't know what's up with me. Maybe I'm just lazy.'

'Dude, you're anything but lazy. You speak a catrillion languages, tutor six hundred kids a week, and you have

46

your makeup Insta on the side. What are you at now, twenty k followers?'

A small quirk at the corner of her lips. 'Twenty-two.'

'Exactly. You're killing the game.'

Gabriela brightens up at this and hoists her backpack further up her shoulder. 'Speaking of, when are you going to let me give you that makeover? I've had the palettes picked out for months. Your cheekbones are going to look insaaane.'

Gabriela's been asking to give me a makeover for ages, ever since she first got into the beauty scene, and it makes me feel kind of weird. I've never been into that stuff, and it feels kind of like she's trying to . . . fix me? Make me less offensive to look at? In any case, no matter how uncomfortable it makes me, I'd never say anything to Gabriela, because I know how much she loves it. She probably doesn't think of it that way at all; she's the least malicious person I've ever met. Still, it's starting to get under my skin.

Is that just friendship, though? Taking an interest in each other's hobbies? Gabriela offered to come to the science museum with me, and we're always listening to Keiko's latest demos, even though neither of us knows much about music. I'm probably just overreacting.

Hell, maybe I *should* let Gabriela work her magic on my face. It's possibly a less drastic measure than taking miracle drugs in order to attract guys. In the cold light of day, I'm giving myself major side-eye for buying those shady motherfuckers.

A few days later, I have AP Physics first thing. I walk in early, because punctuality is the finest quality a human being can possess in the eyes of . . . well, both dads. I distinctly remember playing model trains as a kid, and they made me write out an actual departure schedule – and stick to it. The worst part is that I don't recall ever feeling stifled by this. I enjoyed the rules and the sense of purpose. I guess I was always destined to be a science fanatic. Or a serial killer. But there's time yet.

(FWIW, if I *were* to become a serial killer, my weapon of choice would be a frozen pork chop carved into a point. I would stab my victims to death, then cook and eat the pork chop to destroy the evidence. Anyway.)

The classroom is swelteringly hot, and I'm surprised to find Haruki is already there, sitting at the back of the class. He wears a plain white T-shirt with rolled sleeves, and faded black jeans despite the fierce sun. His pale ochre-brown skin is smattered with light freckles, and his black hair is messy on top, short around the sides. Serving up your basic Hot Guy Lewk.

On his desk is a crisp printout of the same college-level paper I'm attempting this session. Torres must've caved and let him study modern physics too. I kind of don't blame her, because Haruki's parents are library donors and school-board members, but part of me is disappointed. This was . . . my thing. It made me feel special, and I earned that feeling. And now I have to share, even if it is with the most beautiful guy in school/the world.

As I unpack my stuff on the table next to him, Haruki looks over at me. My stomach flip-flops. On second thought, maybe this new common ground will be the thing that *finally* makes him pay attention to me – in the right way, this time. Maybe we'll bond over particularly tricky problems, and share theories over milkshakes at Martha's Diner. Maybe he'll come to MIT too, and we'll be the power couple of the Theoretical Physics Society. We'll name our kids Volta and Galilei, and we'll have a cat named Schrödinger just for the laughs. It's written in the stars, right?

Nope. All that happens as we lock eyes is a smug, self-satisfied smirk, then Haruki turns the first page and starts scribbling in the margins in mechanical pencil.

Any normal person would feel annoyed right now. He's being an immature jerk. But part of me is kind of . . . proud? Haruki is smug to have reached the same level as me. It's a backhanded compliment, in a way. A very, very tenuous way, but still. Let me have this.

The lesson gets underway, and at first I struggle to tune

out the scritching of Haruki's mechanical pencil next to me. I'm hyper-aware of the scent of warm skin and fresh laundry, the bouncing of his knee against the table, the periodic sniffing that suggests his allergies are playing up. It's intoxicating being this close to him, working on the same thing, breathing the same air. (Yep. Definite serial-killer vibes. Please keep me away from the frozen-pork aisle.)

But then my competitive streak takes hold, and I find myself flying through the paper at a rate of knots. If Haruki thinks I'm someone worth emulating, then I have to live up to that. I have to exceed it, even. Almost breathless, I mentally sort through complex equations and mind-bending problems. I'm both invigorated and relaxed. This is how normal people probably feel after sex. Or hot yoga.

As I stop to take a sip of water, though, I notice that Haruki's knee has stopped bouncing, and the pencil has stopped scritching. I glance over from the corner of my eye, and notice that he's peering at my paper, trying to copy the answers.

Resisting the urge to grin victoriously, I realize he's not as smart as he thought he was. But he's too proud to admit he's struggling with the paper, so he's cheating his way through it instead.

I weigh my options. I could cover the page with my arm or pencil-case, and leave him to flounder on his own. Or tell Torres at the end of class, and have her bring his smug ass back down to high-school level. Or use this to my advantage in the whole getting-Haruki-Ito-to-fall-in-love-with-me-and-buy-me-a-kitten-called-Schrödinger mission.

No prizes for guessing which option I choose.

I lift my gaze and quirk the corner of my mouth up in a half-smile, then angle the paper towards him so he can see better. The second he realizes I'm on to him, he quickly looks away, a faint tinge of pink prickling at his cheeks. But then he seems to swallow his pride, and turns back to face me, smiling in the most disgustingly cute and grateful way. He's apologetic and bashful as he rubs the back of his neck. Then he bites his lip, jots down the answer, gives me a slight nod, then turns the page once more.

This may sound like a very minor chain of events, like a millipede waving to pond algae, but as the bell rings and class is dismissed, my blood is roaring in my ears. Haruki wordlessly offers to take my paper up to Torres, and I numbly hand it to him. I feel hot and cold at the same time as the adrenaline pumps through my veins, and I flee the classroom before I can screw up this perfect sequence of affairs.

Next period we have gym, and it's cross-country season despite the lingering summer heatwave. Thanks to my height and gangly limbs, I'm actually a pretty decent runner, but I usually hang back with Keiko and Gabriela so we can chat. I spend the first mile filling them in on this morning's veritable sex fest with Haruki.

'How awesome is that?' I finish, breathless from excitement if not from cardiovascular exertion. I'm basically just power-walking alongside Keiko.

Gabriela grins and yanks up her tiny spandex shorts with a satisfying snap of elastic. 'Very awesome.'

Keiko huffs and puffs, staring angrily at the patchy grass like she wants to murder it one blade at a time. 'Yep. You've basically been to third base.' She pulls her polo shirt up to her head and blots the sweat from her face, taking half her eyebrow powder with it. 'For the love of actual fuck. Cross-country should be illegal. How is this not a war crime?'

I try to make it look like I'm just as exhausted as she is, rearranging my features into a grimace. In reality, my muscles feel loose and strong, like they could sprint forever. Part of me wants to, just to see how it'd feel, but I don't want to leave my friends behind. 'So what should I do now? Should I ask him out? God, what am I saying? Of course I can't. I can barely speak actual words in front of him.'

Keiko hacks up a lung, then says, 'Maybe we could get you one of those robot voices like Stephen Hawking has.'

'Had,' I correct. 'He's dead. And that's highly offensive.'

'To who? Robots? Dead people?'

I pause. 'Unsure. I just know it's not a great voxpop.'

The guys appear over the hill in front of us — they set

off before we do, so start looping back on us before we even reach the halfway point. Leading the pack is none other than Haruki, barely breaking a sweat as his legs pump against the turf.

'Oh god, oh shit, what do I do?' I mutter. Haruki is rapidly approaching, his red shorts a blur as he gains ground fast. Close behind him is Ryan Woods, Gabriela's boyfriend. 'Oh god. Shit. I can't breathe.'

'I know the feeling,' Keiko grumbles, dabbing at her freshly buzzed undercut.

'This might sound radical,' Gabriela says, voice uneven from the effort of jogging. 'But maybe you could consider *not* losing your giant genius mind at the mere sight of him?'

And then he's almost on top of us, and Ryan looks over and nods in a very cute way at Gabriela, and I don't know what comes over me but I make *actual literal eye contact* with Haruki, and, like *some sort of sex pest*, I say, 'Hey.'

Haruki flinches – seriously, an honest-to-god recoil – and speeds up to get past us, without so much as a backward glance. Ryan winks at Gabriela, who giggles unabashedly, and takes off after Haruki.

The snub-induced humiliation must be written all over my face, because Keiko takes a deep, raspy breath and manages to puff out, 'You know what? Screw him. You said it yourself, you're way smarter than him. Hell, than most people.'

A gulping intake of breath. She rips her polo shirt over her head and tosses it to the ground. She's wearing two sports bras – one pink camo, one deep khaki – and vintage gym shorts that hug her curvy waist. 'And you're funny and weird and an all-round awesome human. You deserve better, okay?'

'Exactly!' Gabriela agrees, tucking a loose lock of hair behind her ear. 'Plus you're sweet, and loyal, and generous, and a way, *way* faster runner than us. Not that it's hard. So yup. Screw him.'

A pang of dejection stabs at my gut. I know they're trying to make me feel better. And yet it stings that neither of them included the word 'beautiful' or 'pretty' or even 'cute' in their compliments. Is it so beyond the realms of reality that they couldn't even bring themselves to lie about it?

Maybe those pills weren't such a bad idea.

5

When I get home from school, I'm weirdly not in the mood to study. Usually homework gives me a lady boner, and I have to ration it out lest I accidentally OD on that sweet, sweet ecstasy. I wish I was exaggerating in some way, but it's true. Homework is my jam, my butter, and my toast. But tonight I'm just not feeling it.

After I help Dad make lasagne and mountains of garlic bread for dinner, it's still warm out, so I decide to help Vati with the 'gardening'. I use the term very loosely. When I came home from school, I found half a dozen gnomes pegged to the washing line by their ears, because he'd given them all a bath. In the actual bath tub.

Once Vati has changed back into his denim overalls, we tend to the vegetable garden, which is essentially a selection of grossly deformed and entirely inedible zucchini. Vati had a limited run of success growing basil in the early summer, and got a little cocky thereafter. Tonight we're digging up carrots to see whether any of them are actually safe for human consumption. Sirius lies beside us, panting and blinking against the low sun.

Elbow deep in dirt, Vati rummages around and yanks out a single carrot which looks alarmingly like a cock and balls. A bendy, bulbous cock and balls. With strange little hairs sprouting from the tip.

Vati nods approvingly. 'I am very, very aroused right now.'

It is not an exaggeration to say something inside me dies at this statement. 'Vati, *bitte*.'

'No, *Bärchen*, it is important that we have an environment in which you are comfortable talking about sex. You don't have that? Well, that is the number-one cause of herpes in America.'

I stare down at the dirt I'm kneeling in. An earthworm squirms and wriggles in a very pathos-y kind of way. 'Ugh. It's just weird. Talking about that stuff with you. You're both dudes.'

'That is very sexist and rude.'

'You know what I mean, though. Remember when you tried to talk to me about my period?'

Vati guffaws. 'In hindsight, the visual aid was not wise.'

'You put barbecue sauce in a diaper. So you can see why I don't want to discuss the birds and the bees with you.'

Vati frowns and wipes his forehead on his forearm, leaving

behind a giant smear of mud. 'What does wildlife have to do with anything?'

'Never mind.'

Snapping off his gardening gloves, Vati roots around in the pocket on the front of his overalls. 'Forgive me.'

'For what . . . oh god. *Nein*. Vati!'

He's pulled out a condom. An honest-to-god condom. And he's already tearing through the wrapper. Sirius barks in confusion.

'You pinch the tip, like this.' He grabs the deformed carrot and shoves the condom on the sprouty end. 'And you roll down, see?'

I groan and drop my head into my hands. 'For god's sake. This was premeditated. You actually thought, oh, I will convince my teenage daughter to tend to the carrots with me, and I'll take a condom just in case any impromptu sex-ed opportunities arise.'

'I think you mean "arouse".' Vati laughs hysterically at his own terrible joke. 'Anyway, hopefully any *Schwanz* you encounter will be less bulbous than this carrot.'

I flop backwards into the dirt with a thud, crushing the yellowing cilantro under my back. 'I want to die.'

'At least it won't be from herpes.' He hands me another condom, and a deformed zucchini to practice on. 'Be safe, *Bärchen*.'

Disgusted though I may be, I take the props just to shut him up. 'You have ruined that nickname forever. And also carrots.'

'My apologies.' Vati stuffs the old condom back into his overalls and pulls out something else – a postage slip. 'Oh, I forgot. There's a package for you in the house.'

Despite my lack of core muscles, excitement causes me to sit bolt upright. 'Where?'

'I put it on your bed. You know, I –'

Grabbing the zucchini and the condom, I clamber to my feet, wipe my muddy hands on Vati's overalls, then dash towards the porch doors. 'I gotta go. Try not to molest any more vegetables.'

Breathless after the sprint upstairs, I skid into my bedroom and see the package resting nonchalantly on the bedspread. The brown paper wrapping is discreet and doesn't hint at what's inside – not even so much as a university logo. I prod at it with the deformed zucchini just to be sure it's not on the brink of detonation.

I know I should wait until my dads go to bed before I open it, because I don't want to risk either of them walking in and catching me with a box of murky internet pills in my hands. But something inside me burns to open it. My hands itch, and I can't think of anything else but tearing through the packaging. Is this how chain smokers feel about their next cigarette? Like they'll combust if they don't get it in the next 0.2 milliseconds?

Sticking my head into the corridor, I listen for my dads. Vati's voice drifts through the open hall window. It sounds like he's performing some kind of Punch & Judy show with a family of malformed potatoes, and Dad is watching from the kitchen window, laughing politely at the extremely slapstick performance. I slip back into my bedroom and close the door quietly.

Sitting cross-legged on my bed, I use a pointy nail file to slice through the package seal, and slip my fingers inside. They close around a cool, smooth cardboard box which rattles when I pull it out. All of the information on the packet, including the leaflet explaining potential side effects, is in Portuguese. The pills themselves are small – 10mg at most – and vivid purple. My heart thuds in my chest.

So here it is. The potential solution to all my worldly problems. And I feel . . . I don't know how I feel, exactly.

The overriding emotion is curiosity. Will they actually work? How will it feel if they do? Will I notice an immediate difference, or will they take time to get into my bloodstream? What will it be like to have hordes of admiring fans lusting after me in the cafeteria? Will I suddenly become some kind of egomaniac? Will I start seeing myself differently? Will I be able to look in the mirror without the sinking disappointment that I haven't magically turned into a Hadid sister overnight?

Maybe I'll finally be able to accept myself as I am.

My belly flutters with excitement. My veins fizz with the potential.

Beneath the curiosity, though, there's a curdling sensation. Like nerves, or dread. Something fear-shaped. What if something goes wrong? What if I have an allergic reaction to the pills? Sure, my regular life is dull and often humiliating, but I still want to keep living it. How much would I hate myself if I woke up in the hospital with a shaved head and a scar down my cranium from emergency brain surgery? What if I lost the power of speech, or the ability to walk, or, god forbid, something happened to my tastebuds? A life without ever tasting Dad's brisket again would not be worth enduring.

Oh god, my dads. What if the pills did work – too well? Would my *dads* be attracted to me? Or would their deep-rooted familial love for me override the effects of the pheromones? Is that even a die I'm willing to roll?

Shuddering, I realize I can't do it. Getting Haruki to fancy me is not worth the long list of risks. I've just decided not to take them when I hear footsteps climbing up the stairs. Panicking, I stuff the pills into my school backpack just in time. There's a polite tap at my door – it must be Dad. Vati never knocks.

'Come in,' I call, trying and failing to make my shaky voice sound as normal as possible.

Dad walks in and immediately freezes. That's when I realize I'm still cradling the deformed zucchini in my left hand, the condom perched on the bed in front of me. Dad looks at me, aghast.

'Oh, no! This isn't . . . I'm not . . . Vati, he was giving me a demo –'

'I'll come back later,' Dad mutters, even though he believes both contractions and poor vocal clarity to be signs of a weak mind. He shuffles back out the door, closing it too fast behind him, and practically sprints back downstairs. From a man who is usually so controlled, this is nothing short of bone-chilling.

Sighing deeply, I pull out my phone to text my group chat with Keiko and Gabriela.

Why do vegetables have to be so phallic? It's a serious design flaw.

Gabriela does the crying-laughing emoji, and Keiko replies instantly.

Vegetables have no redeeming qualities. How many times do I have to tell you?

6

Over the weekend, I catch up on my homework, do some extra credit work, help Vati paint the front door eggplant purple, try not to make eye contact with Dad after Zucchinigate, and hang out with Gabriela and Keiko a whole bunch. We go to see the movie Keiko wanted to see, and true to form she did seem incredibly *into* the scenario of rock-star-falls-for-manager. She threatened to cut a hole in the bottom of her popcorn bucket for 'easy access.' At the mention of this maneuver, Gabriela almost vomited everywhere, then disappeared pretty quickly after the movie to grab an impromptu dinner with Ryan.

I don't know why this bugs me so much. The obvious answer is boyfriend jealousy, but I think it's more than that. Lately, it's like something has been shifting in the waters of our friendship with Gabriela, and I can't put my finger on what.

On Sunday, Ryan is mercifully hanging with the guys, so

we head over to Keiko's house so we can help her build a new website for her music. Gabriela styles Keiko with dramatic cat-eye makeup and a thrifted Elvis Costello tee, then I take some headshots with my smartphone camera. In the background, Keiko's latest demo plays over the computer speakers. She's trialling a new Stevie Nicks style and it's . . . hit and miss, shall we say.

Keiko's bedroom is wallpapered floor to ceiling in old record covers, which she's taped together into a mural. There's also a lot of incense from last winter, when she was briefly convinced she was a mage. Unfortunately, she also shares a room with her nine-year-old sister, Momo, and there's currently a turf war between Momo's mermaid merch and Keiko's guitar collection. Momo is away at a soccer tournament today, so Keiko has hung all of the mermaids from the bannister in some kind of mass-execution situation.

Gabriela and I are hunched over Keiko's beat-up laptop, pulling together a rudimentary website design using some cheap software we found. Gabriela has a way better eye for it than I do, and hunts down some free music-themed illustrations to adorn the sidebar. Proud luddite Keiko, who is much too edgy for nerdy things like computers, lies on her bed and scrolls through Instagram. The irony is apparently lost on her.

'Have either of you ever spoken to Samira Hossain?' she

asks, picking at her heavy mascara with her fingernail. 'I'm into her.'

Keiko came out a little over a year ago. She'd been acting out of character for a while, evading questions and generally keeping her giant mouth shut far more often than usual. She was also spending way more time with Katie Michaels, one of Gabriela's cheerleading friends.

The deep-seated paranoia in me worried that she was finally realizing she was much, much too cool to be hanging out with me, and replacing me accordingly. But then I pulled my head out of my rectum and noticed the way she tilted her phone to the side while she was texting Katie, a coy grin on her face. The total lack of interest in the countless guys who hit on her wherever we went. The fact she went to see Captain Marvel three times a week despite declaring superheroes 'the realm of tragic six-year-olds who don't want to be tragic six-year-olds anymore.' (Don't get me started.)

One day she was hanging out at my place, the two of us chilling on sun loungers and watching my dads install a phallic water feature on the lawn, when she blurted out:

'I like girls.'

In that split second, I had a decision to make. I could either say, *no shit, of course you do* — because of course she does — and risk making her feel like the moment she'd built up to for so long didn't matter. Because even though it shouldn't matter, it does, and especially to her. Or I could say something saccharine and cloying, which isn't her at all, and it isn't me either. I shot somewhere down the middle.

'Thank you for telling me.' I wanted to say I was proud of her, because I was, but that would've sounded patronizing.

She slurped her iced tea and turned to me. Vati stroked the water feature lovingly in the background. 'That's it?'

I shrugged. 'What else were you expecting?'

'Honestly, I expected you to ask whether I'm fucking Katie.'

I laughed at her bluntness. It's one of my favorite things about her. 'Are you?'

A heavy eye roll. 'Duh.'

'Have you told your mom?'

Keiko's dad went on a business trip to Japan three years ago and just . . . never came back. She never, ever talks about it. At least not since the day she called me and sobbed down the line for several minutes, before finally choking out that her dad was gone. By that point I was already halfway to her place to perform the Heimlich maneuver, because it really sounded like she was dying.

When I asked about her mom, though, Keiko had her first wobble. She fiddled with the necklace her mom had bought for her sweet sixteenth. 'She's going to hate me.'

Softly, I said, 'She won't.'

'Have you met the woman? She grounded me for a month for sneaking into an R-rated movie.'

'Well, technically that's illegal. Being gay isn't.'

'You know that's not the point.'

'I know.' I squeezed her hand, surprised how sweaty it was. She was obviously more nervous about coming out to me than I thought. 'I'll come with you if you want.'

When Keiko eventually told her mom she liked girls, her mom – a voluptuous nurse with a sailor's mouth – burst into a massive grin and said, 'No shit, of course you do.'

But back to now. 'Samira Hossain. She's a junior, right?' I ask, trying out different fonts on Keiko's new site. 'Track captain?' I only know this because I've seen Samira hanging out with Haruki at lunch. Please do not report me to the authorities for this blatant stalking.

Keiko blows air through her purple lips. 'Yup. Do you think she's gay? Do you get that vibe from her?' A new song starts, and she performs a weird limb-shaking dance from her reclining position. 'Oh my god, I love this song. It's so bouncy.'

Gabriela laughs, taking a sip of Boba tea. 'You wrote it.'

'I know. I'm so talented.' Keiko examines her makeup in her front-facing camera, turning her head so it catches the light in different ways. 'Gabriela, this makeup is killer. Like, forreal. Will you still hook me up when you're working on movie sets in Hollywood?'

Gabriela half-snorts, half-sighs. 'My parents would murder me if I "wasted my brain" being an MUA.'

Keiko shrugs. 'At least you'd die with a killer cut crease.'

'Any idea what you want to do that your parents *would* approve of?' I ask, watching Gabriela dragging Keiko's new headshots into place on the homepage.

'They're old-fashioned. Unless it's medicine or law, it's not worth doing.' Two or three over-aggressive clicks. 'And considering how a) squeamish and b) non-confrontational I am, neither seems like a great option.'

Keiko sits up suddenly. 'Hang on, Samira just posted on her story. Looks like she's hanging out with Haruki and a bunch of other track and field weirdos.' She tilts the phone toward me and Gabriela, holding her thumb on the photo so it stays open. 'Hey, does this pose look romantic to you? Simon Kelly has his arm around her waist, but does she seem into it?'

I squint, but the lighting is dim and Samira's expression is hard to read. 'I can't tell. Lemme do some digging.' I pull out my own phone and load up Instagram.

Then my heart stops.

I have a DM from Haruki Ito.

A hot jolt of adrenaline bursts through my shaking hands as I open the message.

Hey. So this is random. But do you wanna go see a movie or something? Like, as in, a date. :)

I scream. An actual, eardrum-bursting scream. Gabriela drops the mouse in alarm. Keiko shouts back, 'What the fuck!'

'HARUKI ASKED ME ON A DATE!' I squeal, as laughter erupts through my chest. I stare at the message in astonishment, sure I'm dreaming, sure this cannot be real.

Keiko grabs the phone from me and punches the air triumphantly. 'Yassssss! Finally! Oh my god, dude. I'm so happy for you! Are you dying? I would be dying.'

I beam. 'Literally slipping into cardiac arrest at this very second.'

A wave of pure, unfiltered happiness rolls through me. The person I've loved from afar for years finally noticed me. I picture the internet drugs in my backpack, unneeded. I already have everything I need to make guys like Haruki like me. Maybe I *am* enough. Just by being myself, by helping him in Physics and goofily saying hey to him while he was running, I showed him I was fun and chill. And he wants to know more.

Gabriela squeezes my hand. 'This is awesome, Caro. What are you going to say?'

'I mean, yes, obviously!' I giggle. 'But how should I phrase it? Should I leave him hanging for a while? Should

I play it cool, or show how into him I am?'

'Pass it here. I got this.' Keiko grabs the phone and starts typing. A twinge of discomfort plucks at me. What if she accidentally hits send before we're ready? I'd be more comfortable typing stuff in the Notes app first. Keiko looks up, smiling with satisfaction. 'Okay. Sent.'

My stomach plummets through an intestinal trapdoor. 'You sent the message without showing me?'

Keiko shrugs, handing the phone back to me. 'Relax. It's pitch perfect.'

Movie sounds awesome! Salty or sweet popcorn? That's the ultimate question. :)

'I mirrored his emoji usage,' Keiko explains. 'It subconsciously shows you're both on the same page. And the flirty light-hearted question encourages further conversation without being too intense.'

Despite my euphoria at being asked out by Haruki, I can't help but feel a little disappointed. I've waited for this moment for so long, and Keiko just stole a piece of the joy from me. Constructing the perfect text response can be so much fun, and I've just lost out on it. Even though her answer is cute and not embarrassing, it's also not . . . me. And isn't it me Haruki was asking out to begin with?

Gabriela studies my face. I swallow hard, then say, 'That's perfect. Thanks, Keiko.'

Keiko winks. 'What would you do without me?'

Maybe I'm imagining it, but Gabriela looks a little disappointed that I didn't call Keiko out. If I'm being honest with myself, I'm disappointed too. Why can't I be more headstrong? But arguments with Keiko are fierce, and it's usually best to avoid them at all costs.

Anyway, I just have to focus on the good: Haruki Ito asked me out! And I didn't have to take miracle drugs in order for that to happen! And maybe, just maybe, I'm enough after all!

I picture us hanging out in the movie theater, watching the latest Fantastic Beasts release, arms brushing together, flickering lights of the movie dancing across my face. I smile at the thought.

When I look down at my phone, Haruki has replied.

Oh god, I'm so sorry. My asshole friends stole my phone. Please ignore the last message?

It's like being punched in the chest.

Heat burns at my cheeks. I whimper and drop my phone, covering my face with my hands so my friends can't see the tears.

Gabriela picks up my phone and reads. She gasps softly.

'Oh, Caro. I'm so sorry. Are you okay? I swear, if Ryan had *anything* to do with this I'll . . .'

Stupid, stupid, stupid. How could I have been so stupid? How could I have honestly believed someone like Haruki would want to go on a date with me?

'That *dick!*' Keiko fumes, thumping the bedspread with her balled-up fist. 'I'm going to kill him. Actually kill him. How would you like me to do it? The bloodier the better. I think my mom has a chainsaw in the garage.'

I can barely hear her. I wish I could feel the same anger she feels, the delicious righteousness that can patch over any wound, but I don't. I feel hollow and ashamed.

Even though I love my friends, I wish they hadn't witnessed all this. I wish I could just pretend it never happened. I don't want Gabriela's sympathy or Keiko's rage. I just want to rewind two minutes and not scream with joy, not let myself feel that euphoric dream-come-true high. Because experiencing it for real, then having it snatched away moments later, is a thousand times worse than being ignored all along.

'I'll be right back,' I mumble, dabbing at my wet face with my sleeve.

I grab my backpack and run to the bathroom, fumbling for the pills before I've even locked the door. I swallow one, then two, coughing as they stick in my dry throat. Wrenching the cold tap on, I take a long, cool drink, splashing the tears from my face, drying them on the soft towel hanging by the shower.

The pills slide down my gullet, and even though it's not possible, I swear there's a slight tingle as they drop into my stomach.

7

Nothing happens.

I'm both disappointed and relieved. Because even though I spend Monday morning wandering the halls unnoticed, as usual, I'm also not dying in a hospital bed. It was a ludicrous risk to take.

Stupid, really, to think some random pills I bought on the internet could make me desirable. I'm pissed at myself for wasting the money, and even more pissed that I allowed myself that desperate glint of hope. And also pissed that I poured apple juice into my oatmeal this morning. Will the horrors never cease? (It was actually weirdly good. *shrugs*)

I don't have Physics today, so I don't have to see Haruki up close, but every second I hike between classes is spent on a knife edge, praying I don't bump into him or the evil teammates who played that prank. I'm not sure my pride – or what's left of it – could take their mockery. The smirks and elbow jostles as I shuffle meekly past, burning with embarrassment that I fell for something so obviously fake.

Keiko's reply haunts me. *Salty or sweet? That's the ultimate question. :)*

The peppy optimism makes me queasy. I delete the conversation from my account, but it still burns behind my eyes like I'm wearing sci-fi contact lenses.

Luckily, I have an excellent coping strategy for when my emotions are going haywire. I think about black holes.

Black holes are almost impossible to comprehend. You think you understand the theory, but when you start to ask questions, and start to dive a little deeper into the science and math that explains them, it completely melts your brain. At least it does for me.

Black holes were predicted by Einstein's general theory of relativity, which posited that when a massive star dies, it leaves behind a small, dense remnant core. The math of black holes is fascinating, because it takes us deeper than we could possibly go in real life, all the way down to the center of the black hole, the singularity, a point of infinite density.

A black hole is anything but empty space. It has a gravitational attraction so strong that nothing, not even light, can escape. We don't know whether black holes form other universes, but it's possible.

People who say science is boring just aren't paying attention.

But to put my problems into perspective, I don't even

have to go that deep into black holes. All I need to do is think about the sheer size of them, and my brain immediately has a meltdown.

Take the first ever picture of a black hole, captured in early 2019 – the one from a galaxy called Messier 87. That black hole is at least 6.5 billion times larger than our sun.

Six. Point. Five. Billion.

6,500,000,000.

That is incomprehensibly enormous. It dwarfs our entire solar system.

Then I imagine myself standing next to the black hole. Not, like, literally in the event horizon. Just figuratively, in order to compare mass.

We are all so impossibly tiny.

I think of the text again. *Salty or sweet? That's the ultimate question. :)*

Doesn't it seem so irrelevant now?

Physics is like a superpower, I swear.

There's a football game after school against our local rivals, and it's Gabriela's first ever appearance on the varsity cheerleading squad, so Keiko and I promise to come along and watch. As she reminds us approximately once a day, Keiko is super not into balls – 'It works because I don't like football and also I'm a lesbian' – but give her her due, she knows this is a big deal for Gabriela, who's been trying to make varsity for years. So she swallows any feelings she may have regarding balls, and agrees to tag along with me.

We stroll down to the field after final period. The air is still hot and sticky, although there's a cool breeze that blows through every now and again. Keiko, being Keiko, is wearing tight leather-look pants, a gingham pussy bow blouse, and orange-coral lipstick. There's no way she's not six thousand degrees Fahrenheit, but she's so committed to The Lewk that she perseveres. As usual, I feel a little dowdy in my jean shorts and tank top, but at least I have the distinct advantage of not having my insides par-boiled and roasted like Dad's famous potatoes.

We find a spot near the back of the bleachers, partially shaded by the giant elm trees surrounding the field. Keiko whips out a fan from her snakeskin purse and starts urgently trying to cool herself down.

She sees me pursing my lips, trying not to laugh. A bead of sweat rolls down her forehead. Haughtily, she retorts, 'If you even *consider* mocking my fan right now, you're racist and I'm cancelling you.'

My phone buzzes with a text from Gabriela.

gahhh i forgot my lucky hair-tie!! do you still have it from lunch? if yes can you bring it down to the side of the field for me?

I look down at my wrist. Sure enough, the skinny lilac hair-tie with the butterfly beads sits next to my watch.

'I'll be back in a sec,' I tell Keiko. 'Gotta give this to Gabriela.'

'Rude! You know I don't like when you guys hang out without me!' Keiko yells after me.

As I push my way down the bleachers, the kids on the ends of the rows look up at me and frown, and a bubble of anxiety pops in my stomach. For someone who craves attention so badly, I really hate inconveniencing people with my existence.

I make it to the side of the field right as the cheer squad dance out of the locker room, high-kicking and waving royal blue pompoms as though they've never been more excited for anything in their entire lives. The players arrive, and the crowd goes wild, and I realize I've missed my window to give Gabriela her hair-tie.

Instead of traipsing back up to the bleachers, I hover near the side of the field in case there's a brief second of calm in which I can dart over to Gabriela. I know how much she loves this hair-tie. It's her little sister's, and she wore it the day she first nailed her cheer audition, and now she never performs without it.

'Hey, cute shorts!' Marnie Flanders calls over, and it takes me a moment to realize she's talking to me.

My first reaction is to blush furiously and assume she's

being sarcastic. I've worn the same pair of faded denim shorts for like, two years, and Marnie Flanders has never spoken to me in her entire life. But I look up, and she's smiling warmly at me through intense hazel eyes, and I manage to stumble out, 'Thanks!'

There's a blow of a whistle and a thudding kick, and cheers burst through the stands. The game starts. I let out my breath. I survived a successful interaction with the most popular girl in school, and I didn't have verbal diarrhea. Will the wonders never cease?

But then something even weirder happens.

One by one, the players stop playing and start staring at me.

The opposition's quarterback stops mid-sprint and sniffs the air, like a dog tracking a scent. It leads him to my nook between the bleachers, and he peers at me as though I'm an alien from a far-away galaxy. Jen Johnson, a player on the home team, grabs the ball from his hands and tears away down the field, but then gradually slows to a halt as though all her childhood fears have come true and she's waded into quicksand and/or the Bermuda Triangle.

Panicking and flicking her gaze between me and the rest of the team, Jen tosses the ball to Craig, our wide receiver, but he doesn't even attempt to catch it. Because he's staring dead at me. Like almost every other player on the field.

And the look in their eyes is like nothing I've ever seen before. As though I'm all of their sexual fantasies come true at once: Leia in her gold bikini, Emily Ratajkowski as a concept, the smell of a freshly leathered football (or whatever does it for sports fans).

Craig suddenly clutches at his crotch as though he's been shot in the dick and falls to his knees. Two others follow suit.

The opposition's quarterback isn't even attempting to disguise his raging boner. He's just gazing lovingly at me, mouth agog.

'What the fuck!' Jen yells.

I look to one side. The opposition's coach now has his full body pressed against the water cooler, trying to disguise his wood.

Nearly every male player on the pitch is completely incapacitated by their boners, hobbling around and lying flat against the ground in a futile effort to hide their tent poles. Even the ref is out of commission, rendered useless by his furious hard-on.

The crowd whispers in a tense hush, the odd crack of confused laughter echoing through the bleachers. I stand rooted to the ground, frozen in shock.

For a few beats, I wonder what the hell is happening. Has someone played a hilarious Viagra-based prank? Is this a very strange flash mob situation?

Then I remember. I took a double dose of pheromone pills. Shit. Is this me?

Frantically recalling the information in the article, I remember they said each pill was found to quadruple the participants' ability to attract a sexual partner.

Are these dudes eight times more attracted to me than usual??

Maybe I shouldn't have taken two pills. That was, uh, a lot.

Laughter bubbles up in my throat, erupting through my open mouth in a strangled kind of way.

This is a mistake. Craig starts towards me on his hands and knees, as though following the intoxicating scent. A handful of others do the same, one palm clutched around their dongs and the other outstretched as though I'm a mirage in a desert. The trees and bleachers melt away, dissolving into a nuclear wasteland. It's like a scene from *The Walking Dead*, if the zombies' actions were driven not by an insatiable desire for human flesh, but instead by their throbbing whistles.

They start to pick up speed, and I stay frozen to the spot. The opposition's quarterback breaks into a jog, a look of dogged determination in his eyes. It's at this point I start to feel a little scared.

There's a banshee scream as someone sprints down the bleacher steps, yodeling into the wind. Keiko. Running faster than she ever has in her life, she tackles the quarterback to the ground with an oooft – and a whimper.

'Keiko!' Gabriela shouts, racing over to check she's okay.

'Run!' Keiko yells over at me, severely winded. 'But also, please text me to explain, because what the fuck!'

I disappear around the corner just in time to hear Keiko say to Gabriela, 'And this is why I don't date men.'

8

I only intend to run back into the school building, but as soon as my long legs start pumping, I find the burn too delicious to stop. Instead I sprint off campus and down the street in the direction of home, backpack bouncing erratically on my shoulders, lungs throbbing from the exertion. It's tough, and painful, but also extremely invigorating. It clears my mind of the chaos that just unfolded and renews a single-minded focus: getting home.

I'll be able to unpack everything that just happened once I'm back in the refuge of my bedroom.

Miraculously, I make it the two miles home without having to stop once. I mean, my jean shorts have chafed my inner thighs into ground beef steak, but still. I feel proud. And also very, very sweaty. So sweaty I could technically be classed as an amphibian.

The front door is locked, and there's no sign of Vati in the garden – he's probably massacred all living things by this point – and no sign of Dad in the kitchen. They must've popped out for an impromptu date, thinking I'd be out at the game until way later.

Panting heavily, I dump my backpack by the antique umbrella stand in the hallway. There's a frantic scuttle of paws on hardwood flooring, and Sirius appears around the corner with an intense look in his one remaining eye.

Before I can even process what's about to happen, Sirius sprints towards me faster than he has in a good three years, launches himself into the air and slams me into the door back-first. And then he proceeds to dry-hump my thigh, with what can only be described as superhuman levels of gumption. (Humption?)

'Bad dog! Bad dog! No!' I yell, words interspersed with gulps of suppressed laughter.

This only causes Sirius to hump harder.

I summon all my worldly strength and wrench him off me. He falls backwards almost in slow-motion, but the look of extreme arousal in his eye does not fade as he plummets to the ground. He lands the fall with the grace of a jungle cat, turns around and begins humping me all over again.

I decide the only course of action is to run. Fast. Sirius has never mastered the stairs, so if I can just make it halfway up . . .

Side-stepping with karate-master agility, I wrong-foot the

horny old hound and leap up the stairs two at a time until I'm safely out of reach. Panting now more intensely than ever, I yank my phone from my back pocket and type a text to my group chat with Keiko and Gabriela:

Back home. Come find me after the game. (If there is still a game? Has anyone been hospitalized?)

Then, glancing down at my wrist, I fire off another text:

Shit. I still have your hair-tie, Gabs. Fail.

I sit there for a while, catching my breath and watching Sirius fuck the bannister until he can fuck no more. He collapses in a heap at the bottom of the stairs, and I briefly worry I might have killed him. How would I explain that one to the ASPCA?

Forget that. How am I going to explain it to Keiko and Gabriela? Or any of the other hundreds of people who just witnessed the Bonepocalypse?

I don't have time to come up with a decent answer.

Just outside the front door, several voices chat inaudibly. Keiko's hearty laugh and Vati's German guffaw. Gabriela and Dad bringing some sense to proceedings. Despite the situation, hearing them all together warms my heart.

My heart pounds in my throat like a whack-a-mole. Are

84

my dads about to look at me in a new light?

'*Bärchen!*' Vati says. To my enormous relief, there's no trace of anything new in his voice, or in the way he looks at me in a proud fatherly manner. And if he's surprised to see me red-faced and panting halfway up the stairs, he doesn't show it.

'I ran home,' I say quickly, hoping the enormity of that statement will nullify the fact that Sirius is completely KO'd. He gives one half-hearted tail wag at the sound of Vati's voice and goes right back to sleep.

'Are you adequately hydrated?' Dad asks sternly, completely unattracted to me, which is not something I ever thought I'd have to be grateful for. 'With the combination of the above-average temperature, your unsuitable running attire, your lack of cardiovascular training and your alcohol addiction, I estimate your current level of dehydration to be moderate to severe.'

'Alcohol addiction?' Gabriela asks, glitter-painted eyes widening.

'Ignore him,' I mutter. 'Let's go up to my room.'

The three of us pile cross-legged on to my bed. Annoyingly, I am actually incredibly thirsty, but I don't want to give credence to Dad's alcoholism tale.

Keiko and Gabriela look at me expectantly.

'Yes?' I ask, drawing out the inevitable for as long as possible.

Quick. Think.

The only answer that keeps presenting itself is telling them the truth. It's certainly the simplest option. But the truth is so humiliating, so desperately tragic. There are so many layers of shame attached to it. Keiko is constantly broke, constantly scraping together cents to record new songs, and here I am burning serious cash on ridiculous internet pills. Not to mention the danger I put myself in by taking them – the pain I could've caused my dads and my friends alike, should anything have happened.

Plus there's something darker and more selfish simmering below the surface.

I . . . *want* them to think this was all me. I *want* them to stop seeing me as the unattractive friend, the one they want to make over. I *want* them to believe that I'm someone worth loving – not just for my brain, but for everything else too.

Footsteps thud upstairs, and I'm saved for another few minutes.

Vati prances in, carrying a jug of iced tea and three tumblers. He's also wearing a pastel pink apron, which has an even pinker cupcake on the front, its open mouth saying, 'You Bake Me Crazy!' Vati bought it for Dad on Valentine's Day, because Dad is a talented pastry chef and also despises wordplay in all forms. ('Language is not a joke, Felix. It is a science. Would you mix aniline and nitric acid for a joke? No, because you would be dead.')

Vati lays down the tea on my dressing table and starts pouring, ice clinking in the glasses. In his very best Amy Poehler voice, Vati says, 'You see, Caro, I'm not like regular dads. I'm a cool dad.'

'Caro, your dad quotes *Mean Girls*,' Keiko says with a laugh. 'Could he be any more awesome?'

I fold my arms. 'So I'm not allowed to watch brain-rotting rom-coms, but you can enjoy all the Tina Fey you want?'

Vati clutches a hand to his chest as though I've mortally offended him. '*Mean Girls* is not a simply a *rom-com*. It is a work of art.'

I roll my eyes. 'Does Dad know you're wearing his apron?'

'Do you know, I do not think he likes this apron very much. I retrieved it from the trash compactor this morning, like I do every day. It is a fun little ritual. So you guys, what is the 411?'

'Vati. *Bitte*.'

'Okay, okay.' He bends down and yanks a white cotton sock off his foot, then starts waving it in the air like a white flag. Just. Why. 'I surrender. Instead I shall go and prank your father. If you hear screams, do not panic. He's a squealer.'

And then, with a *horrifying wink*, Vati departs.

A squealer. I ask you.

'*Tschüß*, Herr Kerber-Murphy!' Gabriela chirps after him.

'Kiss ass,' Keiko mutters at her, but in a loving way.

'Soooo . . .' Gabriela says, handing me and Keiko our iced tea. 'What was that?'

'What was what?' I ask innocently, taking a ravenous drink and fighting the urge not to drain the entire glass in one pop.

Keiko raises a perfectly shaped eyebrow. 'Armawooden.'

'I've actually been using the term Bonepocalypse,' I reply.

Keiko rolls her eyes. 'Stop stalling.'

Wracking my brain for any possible explanation, I say, 'I'm . . . wearing a new perfume.'

'No you're not,' Keiko says impatiently. 'Miss Dior, every day since you were fourteen, including today.'

I slump back against my headboard, heart rate finally returning to normal after my mad dash home. 'You have the nose of a bloodhound.'

'I do. Now tell us the truth.'

I desperately look to Gabriela for backup, but she's staring at me just as hard. Not in an omg-I-want-to-jump-your-bones way, I don't think, but it's getting hard to distinguish. She isn't clutching her crotch, at any rate, so that must be a victory. 'Sorry, Caro. I want to know too. Ryan was like . . . looking at you funny.'

Guilt twinges in my gut. I truly hadn't thought about that. 'Okay, fine. It was . . . witchcraft.'

'Sure,' Gabriela says with a laugh. 'And I'm a sea mermaid.'

'As opposed to a land mermaid?' I frown.

Keiko sighs in exasperation. 'You're talking out your ass.'

'I'm not! I . . . I found a spell online. On the dark internet.'

'A Pagan spell?'

Oh, god. Why did I hurl myself down this rabbit hole? 'I don't know, exactly. It was supposed to make everyone you meet fall in love with you.'

Keiko lays down her tea and folds her arms. 'Show us.'

'The spell?'

'Yup.'

'Right now?'

'Yup.'

Gabriela looks a bit panicked at this. She chews her chapped bottom lip. 'But I . . . I don't think you should cast it again. It seems dangerous, Caro.'

'It is,' I agree. 'Highly dangerous.' Sirius does three sharp barks downstairs, which means Dad is about to feed him. At least he's still capable of barking after his delirious hump-fest.

'Fine.' Keiko starts plaiting her periwinkle-blue hair. 'Just show us a reenactment. Like on those crime shows when they get actors to recreate armed robberies and such.'

This is going badly. 'But I don't have any more used underwear,' I protest weakly.

'You can have mine.' Keiko goes to undo her leather pants.

'No,' I say quickly. 'I mean . . . from a member of the opposite sex.'

'Homophobe.'

'Where did you get some to begin with?' Gabriela asks.

'Uhhhhh. Boys' locker room.' I'm starting to think maybe this isn't actually less embarrassing than telling the truth.

'I have so many questions, and they're all harrowing.' Keiko wrinkles her nose. 'Just do it – without the skid-marked Y-fronts.'

'File under: rejected Nike slogans.'

Keiko and I both cackle at Gabriela's quip. Being an introvert, Gabriela's the kind of girl who doesn't talk all that much, but when she whips out the occasional one-liners, she's funny as hell.

I see no other option but to improv this spell fandango. 'Give me a sec,' I mumble, taking myself out of the room and downstairs where I can come up with something vaguely resembling an action plan.

Wandering aimlessly around the garden, I try to remember what kind of ingredients Keiko used during her mage phase. Rosemary? Patchouli? Sage? Unfortunately, Vati has murdered all of the above, so I have to make do with what I have. Alongside a metal pail, I grab a malformed eggplant, a few blades of grass, and a particularly wizardy garden gnome. I haul them back to my bedroom with a box of matches and a half-formed idea of what I'm about to do.

When I show the girls the ingredients, however, they are skeptical.

'What's the grass supposed to represent?' Gabriela asks.

Without missing a beat, I say, 'Pubes.'

Keiko spits iced tea everywhere. 'Jesus. You think you know a person . . .'

After I've cranked the window open and shut my bedroom door so as not to activate the smoke alarm on the landing, I light a match and drop it into the pail. I feel a bit bad for setting Vati's favorite gnome on fire, but it looks relatively flame retardant. I'm essentially just barbecuing an eggplant at this point.

An idea strikes me.

'Shit! I forgot something!'

I dash back down to the kitchen and grab a handful of sea salt and the pot of squeezy honey. Dad looks at me like I'm plotting an assassination on the President, but give him his due, he just lets me get on with it. I briefly toy with the idea of telling him I'm making margaritas, but it's really not worth the two-hour lecture on how addiction ruins lives.

Back in my room, I sprinkle the salt over the flaming eggplant, then drizzle it with honey. 'The honey represents femininity, and the salt masculinity.'

Keiko snorts. 'Again, very regressive of you.'

There's a long reverent pause as we watch the eggplant cook.

Gabriela breaks the silence. 'It . . . actually smells really good.'

I beam at her. 'Then you're really going to enjoy the next part.'

Putting out the small fire with a damp cloth, I pull three forks out of my pocket. 'Dig in.'

I'm the first to split the roasted eggplant in half, then carve out some of the caramelized insides and take a massive bite. It is actually pretty tasty, despite the vague hint of burnt grass.

Keiko stares at me. 'Well. That took a lot of unexpected turns.'

I can't fight the grin spreading across my face. 'Delicious though, right?'

Keiko and Gabriela both nod their agreement. 'Delicious.'

We chew for a while until the entire thing is devoured. I use the wet cloth to clean the soot off the wizard gnome, and he seems relatively unscathed.

Keiko studies my face. 'You know I think you're full of shit.'

I nod. 'Fair enough.'

9

That evening, I take one more pill. The regular dosage, this time.

Because as strange and terrifying and hilarious as that ruined football game was, the feeling of power that came with it was like nothing I've ever experienced. And I'm not ready to let go of it just yet. I want to see what it can do. I want to see what *I* can do under its influence.

It takes an eternity to fall asleep. My mind races, reliving the chaotic night. My veins fizz with potential and possibility. I want it to be morning already. I can't wait to be in school as this new desirable person. I can't wait to spend a few days in the shoes of someone like Keiko.

When I do eventually fall asleep, I'm back there.

The house is dank. The walls bleed darkness.

I look around, or try to. The dark shapes around me rarely crystallize, but tonight they do. There's a broken crib, wooden slats hanging loose, and a boarded-up fireplace. An indecipherable mess in the corner.

And . . . a balled-up body?

I squint, but I can't be sure.

My body tries to sweat, tries to cry, but there's nothing left inside.

Somewhere, a door opens.

When my alarm slices through the dream, this time I'm not relieved. I've never seen the room so clearly before. Not the broken crib, not the boarded-up fireplace, not the tangled mess of debris and something more human.

I press my eyes shut, try to coax myself back to sleep, but it's no use. I've always been a morning person, and once I'm awake, I'm awake. I'll never be able to drift off again. Not with my pulse jackhammering this fast.

Entering the school building is like something out of a nineties teen movie. You know, after the girl has undergone a dramatic makeover to conform to society's narrow definition of female beauty. That is my new reality. Except my look hasn't changed a bit. Apart from that, the literal plot of a nineties teen movie.

Heads turn, whispers echo, guys wolf-whistle. Girls look at them like they've gone insane, but then they too turn to stare, and something shifts in their gaze. Gabriela stands to my left, mouth agape, while Keiko looks borderline pissed off to my right. She's wearing a leopard-print duster skirt with a crisp white tee and a pink leather jacket. She looks fierce as hell and yet I'm the one getting all the attention. In my denim overalls and beat-up Chucks.

'That was one powerful eggplant,' Gabriela mutters.

'The urge to "that's what she said" you right now is overwhelming,' Keiko says. 'And damn, Jessica Cooper is staring at you *hard*. I've been sowing that seed for weeks, man, don't you dare take her from me.'

I haven't even made it to my locker when the first proposition lands in my lap.

Oakland Forrest, son of our town's only two hippies, comes up to me and clears his throat. His messy blond hair is tied up in a bun, and his shorts look like they need to be doused in disinfectant and/or quarantined on some sort of nuclear test site.

My eyes narrow. Oakland and I haven't spoken since grade school, when he used to bully me relentlessly for having two dads.

'Hey Caro.' His southern California drawl is grating, considering he was born and raised in Charleston.

'Oakland.' I rummage through my locker for my water bottle, barely looking at him. Gabriela and Keiko stand beside me staring at their phones, pretending not to listen.

'How are you today?' Oakland asks in an overly polite tone.

'I'm fine. Thanks.'

'That's good. I'm really glad.' He shuffles his feet, and his flip-flops smack against the linoleum. 'Listen, I was wondering . . . do you wanna go to prom with me?'

I shoot him a withering look. Or, at the very least, what I consider to be a withering look. 'It's September.'

He laughs nervously. 'No, I know. It's just . . . I figure you're going to get a whole bunch of invites. I wanted to get in early.'

I slam my locker shut, a little surprised by the cresting wave of anger that rises inside me. 'And you think that despite what you did to me in grade school, I'd still want to dress up all pretty and go to prom on your arm?'

Oakland pulls an over-the-top My Bad face. 'Uh, sorry about that. I was just a kid, and being a jerk.'

'Well, I was just a kid and went home crying every night, so.' My words are tight and taut like a coil, as though the tears are still lodged in my throat nearly a decade later.

He shrugs, trying to get back to his casual comfort zone. 'Maybe I was just being mean to you because I liked you.'

Ah yes, the not-at-all toxic notion that abusive behavior is a sign of deep-rooted affection. Love it. Huge fan.

'I don't want to go to prom with you, Oakland.'

As he walks away dejectedly, the word 'sorry' tries to

force its way up my throat. It flashes in neon lights in my brain, blasts in a thousand decibels through my eardrums. My every instinct urges me to apologize to him. But I hold firm. For once.

'That. Was. Awesome.' Gabriela's eyes are shiny with excitement, and maybe something a little pride-shaped. I feel a surge of warmth for my sweet, kind friend. I would hug her, but physical affection makes us both deeply uncomfortable, so I settle for a grin.

'Hard agree.' Keiko grins. 'I'm a big fan of Bad Bitch Caro.'

The rest of the morning is an avalanche of attention. I come out of Calc to find sixty new Instagram followers and two more prom invites stuffed in my locker. The single-pill dosage seems to be the sweet spot – if any of them have boners, they do a good job of disguising them.

It feels like sunshine on bare skin after a long winter. I know that sounds tragic, but when you've spent your entire adolescence starved of romantic affection, the sudden influx is a rush like no other. It's like a good dream I never want to wake up from.

So far, I'm having a little trouble figuring out the rules. In the beetles, the pheromones only worked on the male of the species, but it seems a lot more complicated in humans.

From what I can tell, in humans the pheromones can boost attraction for every sex, but that attraction has to have been viable to start with – i.e. only for groups who are normally into women. So like, straight girls and gay guys are still interested in me, but not in a sexual way. Just like, *I've never noticed her existence before, but now I'm looking up as she walks past.*

I don't know. It's complicated.

Far from getting bored, I really come into my own by lunchtime. There's already a higher tilt in my chin, a bouncier spring in my step. I enjoy the sensation of meeting a guy's eyes just to watch his quivering reaction, and the moment when a small altercation seems to break out at the water fountain as two freshmen argue over who has a better shot with me. This feeling is pure power.

As we're eating our chili fries, I struggle to focus on the whole food-to-mouth thing.

'Oh my god, Aziz is staring at me,' I say, making no effort to wipe away the chili dribbling down my chin. 'And Aaron is getting pissed because Aziz is staring at me. This is wild.'

'I mean, it's only because of the spell, right?' Keiko says. She picks at her fries like a small bird. 'It'll stop once the eggplant wears off.'

I raise an eyebrow in a friendly way. 'I thought you said I was full of shit.'

Keiko shrugs, not meeting my eye. 'Well, it's gotta be something.'

'Maybe it's the overalls,' Gabriela says earnestly, god bless her heart.

Someone clears their throat behind us, and I swivel on the bench. Marnie Flanders. *Smiling*. At me.

'Hey, girl,' Marnie says, tucking a lock of auburn hair behind her cuff earring. 'Do you wanna come sit with us? Gabby, you come too!'

I would probably enjoy this moment if Keiko didn't look like she'd been slapped.

To be honest, though, general popularity was never exactly my goal with the pills. It was to entice Haruki into being my boyfriend; to find myself in a loving relationship with someone who adores me. Not to suddenly be seen by the Populars. So while I'm not exactly tempted by Marnie's offer, it's still nice to be asked.

'Oh, I'm good here thanks,' I say, matching her warmth. 'But that's really sweet of you.'

'Actually, I may go sit with the squad, if that's okay?' Gabriela asks, shooting a sideways look at Keiko as though worried she's about to be snarked at.

'Whatever.' Keiko shrugs.

'Go for it,' I add, although I have to admit, I'm a little put out too.

After lunch, it's the class I've been looking forward to all day: Physics. The moment I'll see Haruki for the first time since taking the pills. My heart pounds with anticipation. Is he finally about to notice me for real? No pranks, no annoyance over my special treatment. Just . . . noticing me as a person who might be worth talking to?

I'm the first student to arrive, because obviously, and I take my usual seat at the back. Torres is prepping for the lesson at the front, and we chat a little about MIT and my letter of recommendation. So when Haruki strolls in, I look like even more of a teacher's pet than usual.

But that doesn't stop him visibly recoiling when he sees me. Not, like, in a grossed-out way. More like a . . . *whoa, I think I'm seeing you for the first time* kind of way. My heart fizzes like an Alka-Seltzer tablet in my chest. His perfectly smooth cheek dimples as he smiles, and his deep brown eyes twinkle in a way that makes me melt.

Yes, yes, yessssss. We're on. It's on.

He is, at the very least, noticing me. He might not act on it, and I might completely fuck it up if he does, but this is a good start.

He pulls up the chair next to me, but I don't address him. Not yet. I want this to be on his terms. I want him to feel the desire to look at me, talk to me, be near me, and I want him to have to act on it.

Everyone else arrives and class starts, and I'm doing a pretty good job of ignoring him until . . .

'Pssst.' Those twinkly eyes pierce mine.

I resist the urge to grin like a lunatic. Casually as I can muster, I say, 'Hey.' Ground-breaking, I know.

He gestures to the college paper we're both doing and whispers, 'Do you actually, literally understand this?'

'I actually, literally understand it.' I shrug, like it's no big deal, when in reality my Alka-Seltzer heart is about to leap out of my chest and slam into the back of Maria Lopez's head.

'Damn.' His voice is kinda croaky and deep. 'How'd you get so smart?'

Smirking, I say, 'I listened when Torres talked.'

Ah, there she is. Hermione Granger, queen of flirty banter.

'Fair enough.' He looks down at the paper, then back up at me, then starts twiddling the end of his mechanical pencil. 'Hey . . . maybe you could explain it to me over milkshakes sometime?'

THIS IS IT. IT IS HAPPENING. HOLYYYYYYY —

I cannot believe it. I cannot believe it. If I'm dreaming, please don't wake me up.

The first step of Operation Schrödinger's Cat is underway: bonding over particularly tricky problems, sharing theories over milkshakes at Martha's Diner. Next up: he applies to MIT too, and we become the power couple of the Theoretical Physics Society. Volta and Galilei, we're coming for you.

Somehow, I keep it nonchalant, which I have never

101

before been capable of where Haruki is concerned. I remember what Keiko said, about light-hearted questions. 'That depends. What's your milkshake of choice? There's only one correct answer.'

'Yikes, no pressure.' His forehead crinkles as he considers this. 'Uh . . . chocolate.'

'Oooooh, he strikes out.'

'Wait! No!' He's struggling to keep his voice a whisper now. 'What's the right answer?'

'Vanilla,' I say simply, jotting down an equation on my paper.

'You *have* to be kidding me.'

As I write, I defend one of my more passionate religious beliefs. 'Look, vanilla gets a bad rep. It's used as an insult, an allegory for plainness, but it's perfectly sweet and creamy, with a hint of umami, and just generally all-round awesome, okay?'

'Wow. You really feel strongly about milkshakes.'

'Anyone who doesn't is an idiot.'

Haruki smiles his goddamn perfect smile and says, 'So is that a yes?'

'Excuse me?'

'Will you go out for milkshakes with me?'

I allow a long enough pause for him to sweat, then bite my lip to stop the disbelieving laughter falling out. 'When?'

He shrugs and lays down his pencils. 'I'm free right now.'

'We're in Physics,' I hiss. Ms Granger, the doctor will see you now.

He makes a *pfft* noise. 'No shit, Gracie Hart.'

I gape at him. 'Gracie Hart?'

'From *Miss Congeniality*.'

'No, I know who she is. But isn't the phrase "No shit, Sherlock"?'

'Please. Sandra Bullock would kick that crusty old English dude's ass any day of the week.' He says this with the exact same level of passion I used to defend vanilla milkshakes, and it's . . . extremely attractive. There's a weird throbbing in my lower belly.

Giggling now, I mutter, 'I can't cut class.'

He holds his hands up in defeat. 'Okay, Little Miss Honor Roll. After school?'

'Sounds great, Little Mister Prom King.'

Holy shit.

Holy shit, holy shit, holy shit.

I want to marry these miracle pills. I want to bottle this feeling, except I'll never have to save it for a rainy day because as long as I have these drugs, I'll be invincible. I'll get everything I ever wanted, and then some.

People say you can't have it all. And up until now, I really believed my trade-off for a giant brain was below-average looks and little to no self esteem. When I pictured my future, I always imagined myself pioneering earth-shattering research – but coming home to an empty house.

But no more. I *can* have it all. And I intend to grab it with both hands.

After class, I bound over to Keiko's locker like actual Bambi, fighting the urge to shriek and squeal. She and Gabriela are touching up their lipstick, but both stop dead when I leap in front of them and say: 'Haruki asked me out!'

'No fucking way!' Keiko grins, smacking her violet lips together. 'Get it, gurl!'

'That's amazing, Caro!' Gabriela says, but she looks a little worried. 'And please forget all the stuff we said about him before, okay? He seems great, and if he's into you, that's all we care about.'

My lovely sensitive friend. She's too precious for words. 'Oh, don't worry Gabs. I know you were just having my back.'

Keiko rearranges her bangs in her jewelled pocket mirror. 'So, what are you going to wear? Do you want Gabriela to do your makeup?'

'Nope,' I say simply. 'And I'm wearing this. We're going straight after school.'

Keiko laughs. 'I admire your confidence.'

'Is that a backhanded compliment?' I frown.

'No!' she says quickly. 'Forreal. It's nice to see you feel

comfortable in your own skin for a change. I want more of this Caro.'

I smile back, warmth spreading through my chest. 'Long may it last!'

And it will. It will, it will, it will. Because science has my back. And so do my friends.

Thank you, Professor Pablo Sousa. Thank you.

10

The entire stroll into town smells of barbecues and hot sidewalks. The sun is warm on our faces, even though a few defiant leaves have begun to turn orange.

As I walk past, a group of sophomores playing softball in the park all stop to stare at me. Haruki puffs his chest out, as though he's never been more proud to be seen with the physics geek of the East Coast. This is all, surely, an elaborate dream.

When we arrive, the diner is pretty empty, since basically everyone is outside enjoying the late summer sun. The windows are yawning open to let the pleasant air in, but the diner still smells of pancake batter and crispy bacon.

'So, what's your deal?' Haruki asks, once we settle into a window booth and order two vanilla milkshakes. Victory, thy name is Caro.

I rearrange the straps of my tank top beneath my denim overalls. 'How do you mean?'

'Like . . . where'd you grow up, what is your family like, what are your hobbies?'

An upbeat acoustic song starts playing over the speakers. 'I grew up over on Laurel with my two dads and my cockapoo, Sirius.'

Haruki grins, all dimples and white teeth. 'Nice. From Harry Potter?'

'What's Harry Potter?' I ask innocently.

'Just a small, niche franchise. I wouldn't expect you to have heard of it.'

I snort. I'm kind of surprised by how not-nervous I am. By removing the fear of failure or rejection, the pills are giving me an extra layer of confidence. 'Okay, hobbies . . . I'm in chess club, because nerd life, but I'm not really any good at it. Um, I like gardening with my dad. Watching my best friend Keiko sing.' I'm only just starting to realize how few hobbies I have. At least ones that I do just for me, not because they're what the other person wants to do – or what I feel like I *should* be doing. 'I really want to try running,' I blurt out. 'I think I could be really quick.'

Haruki tilts his head to one side. 'Oh yeah? I mean. Makes sense. You got those long limbs going on.'

HE HAS NOTICED THE PROPORTIONS OF MY APPENDAGES. THIS IS NOT A DRILL.

'Exactly! I know I always hang at the back,' I hurriedly

explain. 'But that's just because my friends hate cross-country.'

Our milkshakes arrive, and I take a long sip. It's creamy and sweet, made with real vanilla pods. Even Haruki gives it an approving look, like dayyuuuummm.

'Your friends seem cool, though,' he says, and I'm weirdly disappointed the conversation moved away from me so fast.

'You know them?'

'Yeah, well, obviously Ryan's obsessed with Gabriela. They're joined at the hip. Have been since he saw her at the beach in what was it . . . summer before freshman year?' An eye-roll that's not entirely genuine. 'He's shallow like that.'

This kind of makes me cringe. Like, I know Gabriela is a supermodel. There's no need to bring it up on this . . . date, or whatever.

Still, I'll never not defend the honor of my friends. 'Luckily she's a pretty great person too.'

Haruki stirs what's left of his milkshake with a jumbo paper straw. He's already devoured, like, eighty-five percent of the delicious nectar of the gods. 'And my sister's a big fan of Keiko's band.'

I groan. 'So I'm the only unknown entity.'

'Uh, no.' He meets my eyes and smiles. 'You're Physics Genius Girl.'

'I'll take it,' I concede.

A sparrow flies full-tilt into the window pane. Haruki screams. Like an actual, high-pitched banshee scream. I immediately begin laughing uncontrollably.

'So you and your friends . . . you seem really different.' He ruffles his hair, which is kinda disheveled thanks to the heat and the unmitigated shock of a rogue sparrow. 'Like in high school, people mostly hang out with other people with the same interests, you know? Theater nerds, football jocks, whatever. They stick in their genre. Whereas you guys are all so individual.'

My already damaged ego flinches at this. Is he hinting that I'm not as cool as my friends? Or am I just unbelievably paranoid at this point? Seriously, nobody ever give me weed. I would call the cops on my own shadow.

'Yeah, I mean we've been inseparable since middle school,' I explain. 'And while we do dabble in other groups, like chess and cheerleading, we just . . . like each other, I guess. Although we do revel in lightly bullying each other.'

'Like how?' Haruki asks.

I show him some of the five million messages I've received from Keiko in the group chat in the last twenty minutes.

Delighted to announce that I have now learned Beyoncé's entire Homecoming set by heart. Shall perform it for y'all

this weekend. Please bring racially insensitive headdresses to complete the authentic Coachella experience.

Caro, you are not allowed to participate in the race jokes on account of how white you are.

WWII sucked and all, but you're not actually Jewish and thus have never been oppressed. Vati is fair game.

'That's hilarious,' Haruki says, and I can tell his laughter is genuine.

'It's just easy when we're together,' I say. 'And yeah, we're all different. Everyone's individual, you know? We just embrace it more.'

A weird expression flits across his face. 'You're making me jealous.'

'In what way?'

He pauses to figure out his words. A new song starts, and something clatters back in the kitchen. The croaky voice of an old woman swears fluidly and excessively.

'Sometimes I feel like my guy friends are all carbon copies of each other,' he mumbles, suddenly unsure of himself. 'We all do sports, all play video games, we all drink and watch NFL and hook up with girls on weekends.' This last part makes me blush, or cringe, or something. 'And, like, I know they all must have things they're secretly interested in outside of that stuff. I definitely do. But it's like nobody will stick their head above the parapet and be like, actually, I'm passionate about this thing.'

Now it's my head's turn to tilt. 'What's your secret interest?'

The conversation is somewhat interrupted when a large plate of waffles arrives in front of me.

'We didn't order –'

The pink-haired waitress rolls her eyes and says, 'From my colleague Stu.' She gestures at the waffles, which I now notice are adorned with a maple-syrup penis, and whipped cream to represent . . . well. 'By colleague, I mean immature fuckbucket. Uh, except I'm not supposed to swear at customers anymore. So . . . frickbucket. Anyway. Please don't dock my tip.'

Haruki splutters milkshake everywhere as I giggle at the plate, for lack of anything better to do. I snap a pic and send it to the group chat, accompanied by the eggplant emoji. Then I grab a fork and dig in.

Haruki stares at me in astonishment/horror. 'You're not actually going to eat those, are you?'

'It's not a real dick, Haruki,' I say earnestly. 'And you should never turn down free waffles. Anyway, I haven't forgotten my question. Secret interest, please.'

Haruki grimaces and stares out on to the street. A lanky girl who can't be any older than eleven dribbles a soccer ball down the sidewalk, weaving in and out of disgruntled pensioners. 'You can't laugh at the dorkiness.'

'Girls don't really do that,' I say, through a mouthful of fluffy waffle. 'Gabriela could tell us she crocheted sweaters for wood pigeons and we'd be like, cool, show us!'

'Okay.' He begins studying the menu intently, as though it's some kind of religious text. Maybe it is. I don't know how strong his beliefs are regarding burgers. 'I can't believe I'm telling you this, but . . . I used to love HEMA.'

I blink. 'The what?'

He looks a little bit like he wants to die. 'Historical European Martial Arts.'

'Oh, like swordplay?'

'Exactly. I . . . did it all the time as a kid, went to tournaments all over the state with my uncle and cousin. And I really miss it.'

'So why'd you stop?'

'I dunno.' He frowns. 'I just became fifteen and self-conscious and . . . stopped.'

I gape at him in disbelief. 'You, Haruki Ito, are self-conscious?'

'Uh, yeah? Why'd you say it like that?'

I laugh, and can't stop the following words from spilling

out: 'Do you have no awareness of how hot you are?'

Gahhhh. Why, Caro?

But Haruki barely seems to notice the blatant thirst klaxon. 'I mean . . . guys don't really care about that. If you want to impress other dudes, it's about how you act, not how you look.'

I nod in fake understanding. 'Masculinity sounds very tiring.'

He shrugs, like, what are you gonna do? Then says, 'Anyway, what's your deal?'

I lay down my fork, having absolutely demolished the dick waffles. 'You already asked me that.'

Now it's his turn to look a little nervous. 'No, like . . . your *deal*. Are you single?'

'Eternally.'

Why did I have to say this? What is wrong with me? Just when I'm beginning to forge a reputation as the hottest property in North America, why point out my past as a sexual pariah? Should I just come right out and say I've had more intercourse with the showerhead than any actual human beings?

'Okay, so . . . do you want to hang out again sometime?' He grins. 'Because I'm very aware we didn't talk about physics, like, at all.'

My heart soars. Is this actually happening? Have I just spent a half hour in Haruki Ito's company, being completely and utterly myself, and now he wants to know more?

I mean, okay, so the pills lured him here. I know that, and so the win is hardly mine to claim. But I do think our connection was real, beneath all the pheromones.

When I say, 'Yes, I would love that,' I want to drink the moment in like the tallest, creamiest milkshake in the world.

11

The next day, I only see Haruki once in school, but he smiles and says 'Hey' when we pass each other in the corridor. Instead of mocking him, like they probably usually would, his friends just look impressed and vaguely jealous. My pride feels like a helium balloon about to burst, straining against my ribcage and living me up off the ground.

The loving attention from the rest of the school population only proves to escalate. And I do mean the rest. Not only do I gain a bona fide posse of fans who follow me down the hallways, I also find myself cringing in my high tops when a couple of male faculty members stare at me in a not entirely teachery way.

Coupled with the fact that this morning, someone crashed into a stop sign as I walked past, I'm learning very quickly that romantic attention is not actually universally positive. There are definitely creepy aspects to it. Another unexpected one is that the pills seem to work on freshmen, and there's something a little skin-crawling about having fourteen-year-olds be super into you. I'd imagine if you're someone like Keiko, who's used to having fans of all ages, it wouldn't be a big deal. But I'm entirely new to having people look at me in that way, and it's taking some getting used to.

Still, the knowledge that Haruki Ito is into me is more than enough to offset the slightly less pleasant aspects of the pheromones.

Keiko walks me to chess club after final period, as usual. And, as usual, we talk about her music. She's busy sharing her eighty-two-point plan for world domination, which begins with sending demo tapes to east coast managers, and ends with performing a duet with Nicki Minaj. I have heard this plan in excess of five hundred times.

As she talks, all chirpy and fast, irritation pricks at me. While Gabriela demanded all the details of my milkshake date as we walked to study hall this morning, Keiko still hasn't asked how it went. Maybe she's just obsessed with passing the Bechdel test, and maybe she just can't relate because she's not really the dating type, but it leaves me feeling a little deflated.

The second there's a pause for breath in her diatribe, I interject with, 'Hey, aren't you going to ask me about my date with Haruki?'

This catches us both off-guard. I *never* interrupt Keiko. So this is kind of an out-of-body experience for me. My soul has escaped through my earhole and is hovering above the situation, howling in warning.

Keiko blinks, her glittery mascara glinting under the strip lighting. 'I mean, I just assumed it went well when I saw the dick waffles.'

'It did,' I say, staring at my feet. I'm already regretting the minor confrontation, as is my soul, which is now mimicking an air-raid siren. 'But don't you want to know what we talked about? Whether we kissed?'

Keiko grins in a you-sly-dog sort of manner. 'Did you?'

'No. But still.'

'Okay.' A slightly awkward pause. She scuffs her Doc Martens along the linoleum. 'What did you talk about?'

I look up at her, inspiration striking for how to get her back on side. 'You came up, actually. His sister is a fan.'

She puffs out her chest exaggeratedly. 'Sounds like I'll make it to point six on the world domination plan sooner than previously thought. Are you going out again?'

'Yup!' I grin. 'To the movies on Saturday.'

Keiko smiles. She looks like she might be about to squeeze my shoulder, but thinks better of it. 'I'm really happy for you, dude. I know you've crushed on him forever.'

I smile warmly. This is all I needed from her. 'Thanks, Kiks.'

We walk past Emily and Ethan, the Griffin twins, as they pin a poster to the noticeboard outside the auditorium. This time, Emily still stares at Keiko as she passes, but Ethan gazes at me, transfixed. Keiko frowns at him, and then at me, like something has changed and she doesn't entirely like it.

We arrive outside chess club. 'Go kill some kings, or whatever.'

Surprise surprise, Mateo is waiting for me inside. He's already set up the board, claiming white for himself.

The difference this time is that when I walk in, almost everyone in the room stops and stares at me. And for some reason, this time it makes me feel weird. It's one thing to trick the jocks and the cheerleaders into thinking you're attractive, but entirely another to con your own people. Plus, I was kind of ready for a break. Just to play chess and be normal Caro for a bit.

The classroom is stiflingly hot. I pull back my chair and flop down opposite Mateo, who gazes at me in a way he has never looked at anything before.

'There's something different about you,' he murmurs reverently.

I smirk, still kind of enjoying the feeling of having a little power over him. 'Nope.'

'There is. Did you cut your hair?'

'That must be it.'

He barely looks down as we glide through the opening few moves. Muscle memory kicks in, guiding him to castle his king and develop his knights, but there doesn't seem to be any kind of thought process going on behind his eyes. He's too busy staring at me, equal parts suspicious and aroused.

I set up my pieces like I always do – in an almost impenetrable fortress. Mateo is distracted enough to leave his dark-square bishop hanging, so I grab that with my knight. It leaves a small gap to my king, but Mateo doesn't capitalize on it, and starts maneuvering a set piece I've seen him play a thousand times before. Not only do I manage to block it, but I manage to capture a couple pawns and his light-square bishop too.

Then I have a decision to make. I can either move my pieces back to where they were before, or use the advantage I've given myself to do what I *never* do and go on the attack.

A slightly hazy Mateo grows impatient as I study the board, weighing my options. I so rarely think offensively that I struggle to see the potential at first. But slowly, I come up with a plan. A way to force him to move in a certain order, leading to a queen-king pin, then a fatal rook-to-A8 finisher.

The buzz as I execute my plan is electric. Mateo realizes his fate a few moves in, but by then it's too late – he's a rat who's backed himself into a corner, with nowhere to go but the trap set for it. I deal my killer blow and grin triumphantly.

'Good game,' he says, but it's not begrudging. It's flirtatious. And it causes the reality of the win to smack me in the face.

Is this a real victory? The pills gave me an unfair advantage. Mateo was distracted and off his game. Then again, I'm the one who used the initial edge the pills gave me and spun it into something real. I was more daring, less apologetic. I put my pieces – and myself – out there.

Still, I walk out of the classroom feeling a little like I cheated on a test. Not that I'd ever know what that felt like, but you know what I mean.

A small voice in the back of my head tells me, 'You don't deserve this.'

I arrive home to a snoozing Sirius, and two dads having a heated conversation in the kitchen. They don't seem to have heard the front door click shut. I hover in the hallway and listen, even as Sirius wakes from his slumber and begins silently humping my knee.

'Michael, you must follow your dream,' Vati says passionately. 'Writing this book, it is your life's purpose. You will change the game for diabetes sufferers the world over. And that is where the dog is buried.'

'Sirius is deceased?'

'Ah, *nein*, maybe another German idiom. It is, how

you say, the heart of the matter.'

Dad sighs. The grandfather clock in the hallway ticks aggressively. 'Felix, my sabbatical is coming to an end, and so is my funding. It is not a responsible course of action to extend my leave of absence.'

'Responsible, responsible, always you are concerned with the responsible —'

'Well, one of us has to be.'

Vati lets out a long, slow whistle. 'That, Michael, is a real kick in the dick. A knock in the bollocks. A punch in the gooch.'

'There is no need to resort to vulgarity.' Dad's voice is getting quieter, which is how I know he's getting annoyed.

'You are a tenured professor.' I can practically see Vati's elaborate gesticulation, even though he's in another room. 'If money gets too tight, you go back to work. It is no big deal. They cannot fire you, that's the beauty of it. You could go into the university in your underpants and they would just have to say, oh, he is a beautiful genius, we must respect the underpants. They must give you an extra sausage.'

'Thankfully I am aware of that particular expression, and I know you are referencing "special treatment", not . . . well, Caro would be amused. The two of you have minds in the gutter.'

True to form, I snigger in the hallway.

'Ah, Caro.' Vati's voice softens. 'That is what this is all about, *ja?*'

A taut pause. 'I would like her college experience to be the happiest, most fulfilling years of her life. If she spends most of the time worrying about money, it will make the program difficult to enjoy to its fullest potential. She should get a job alongside her studies, of course, but I would also like to have a pot of money put aside in case she ever finds herself out of work and short on rent.'

My heart pangs. He's putting his book-writing dream on hold to support me.

'She will be okay,' Vati insists. 'Of this I am sure. Our daughter is smarter and more hard-working than both of us combined, and if you do not realize this . . . well, Michael, I am afraid you have tomatoes in your eyes.'

'Felix, I beg of you —'

I tiptoe upstairs, dabbing at my wet eyes with the sleeve of my shirt.

That night, I have the dreams again. The same as before — the broken crib, the boarded-up fireplace, the curled-up body in the corner of the dank room.

I'm torn between wanting to know more and wishing I could leave this particular truth behind. I love my life. I love my dads. I don't need answers. I don't need the details of this part of my life, because it has no bearing on who I am today. My mother gave birth to me, and then . . . and then . . . I don't know.

Maybe that's too big a thing to not know. Maybe it'll remain an open wound until I can close it with knowledge.

Yet the only way to acquire those memories is by asking my dads, and the thought breaks me. I don't ever want them to think they're not enough. I don't ever want them to think I'm going to abandon them and seek out my birth mother instead. They have given me everything I ever wanted and needed, and then some. They have adored me and cared for me and argued over me. They're my world, and my love for them is bottomless.

I lie awake until sunrise. These flashbacks are a thorn in my consciousness; a blade wedged in a rift, threatening to crack it wide open.

The week blazes by in a haze of adoration. And it's weird, because I don't seem to get used to it at all. In fact, I find it harder and harder to wrap my head around as the days go on. When I walk down the hallway followed by a sea of eyes and whispers, it's like I'm watching a celebrity I don't know striding down the corridor.

Sometimes the feeling of being seen is pleasant, like a refreshing breeze of validation, while other times I find it a little claustrophobic. When you're used to fading into the background, suddenly being thrust into the limelight – even when it's by your own doing – is extremely jarring. It's like riding an adrenaline high for days at a time; it's a high, yes, but after a while it makes you feel jittery and a little spiky.

Still, I can't deny that the surge in Instagram followers and multiple prom invites feels good. If that makes me shallow, so be it. Plus there's the fact countless people keep offering to do things for me – carry my books, bring me coffee, hire me to tutor them. The small kindnesses I so desperately wanted from a relationship, except from dozens of people at once. It's overwhelming.

Throughout the hysteria, I manage to stay on top of my schoolwork, keep pushing forward with my MIT application, and hang out with Keiko and Gabriela when we're not participating in our respective hobbies, and when Ryan's too busy to chill with Gabriela. I 'garden' with Vati, cook with Dad, Skype with Leo to discuss how college is going, and visit my grandma at the dementia care centre downtown. Grandma's nurse – a young, attractive woman called Ana Sofia – spills lukewarm carrot and coriander soup down my grandmother's wrinkled cleavage the moment I open my mouth to talk. Vati finds this extremely funny. Dad does not.

Haruki and I hang out a bunch during lunch, and Physics becomes our own private nerd club as we work through our college papers at the back of the classroom. Being around him is becoming more and more comfortable, and I can feel the real warmth of kinship beginning to grow between us. We actually have way more in common than I realized, like an obsession with elephants and a penchant for cinnamon rolls. Once he finds out the latter, he starts bringing me a fresh one every morning. It's a small thing, but it feels warm and significant. I remember how much I envied Gabriela for her fresh egg and cheese bagels delivered by Ryan, and I smile, promising myself I'll never take it for granted.

I beat Mateo a few more times at chess, which gives me enough confidence to take on Tara Black, the reigning state champ. She's ace and doesn't seem all that affected by the pheromones emanating from me. I still haven't figured out the exact rules of the drugs, but it seems to only magnify attraction that was feasible to begin with.

Anyway, I get absolutely hammered by Tara, of course, but I actually try some interesting moves and catch her off-guard a few times. Despite the loss, I leave the match feeling invigorated and motivated to keep pushing myself out of my castled comfort zone – and eventually win a game against someone who isn't drooling at the mere sight of me.

Today is also Ryan and Gabriela's anniversary, and even though she knocked it out the park with his gift – tickets to see his favorite comedian perform in the city – he truly outdid her this year. He made the enchanted rose from *Beauty and the*

Beast, complete with glass dome and fairy lights, then carved the date they met on the wooden base. It's a little rough around the edges, being homemade by a jock with very little artistic flair, but it's beyond sweet. He knows that's Gabriela's favorite Disney movie.

When I see the rose, the edge of jealousy isn't as sharp as usual, but it's there. I still want what they have, and I still feel years away from getting it. I wish I could fast-forward the weird dating stage and get to that point with Haruki.

On Friday morning, I close my locker to see Haruki standing on the other side of it, dressed in a deep red T-shirt, black skinny jeans and box-fresh white sneakers. He seems both super chill and a little nervous. My heart performs some kind of lindy hop. Even if I keep taking these drugs, surely it will *never* feel normal to see him so close to me.

'Hey,' he smiles, cheeks dimpling sweetly as he does. He holds out a still-warm cinnamon roll, and it smells divine. 'Whaddaya think about inviting Ryan and Gabriela to the movies with us?'

'Like a double date?' I say, spraying pastry everywhere in a very hot way.

'Yeah! If that's cool?'

Despite a brief flicker of disappointment that I won't get him all to myself, I grin and lick the sugar off my lips. 'Sure. I'll ask her if she's into it.'

Haruki pulls out his phone, presumably to text Ryan. 'Awesome.'

Before I can stop myself, I blurt out, 'Wait. Was Ryan the one who stole your phone?' I've wanted to ask this for a while, but I didn't want to make Gabriela feel awkward if it was.

'When?' Haruki asks, but from the embarrassment in his dark eyes, I know he knows exactly why I'm asking.

'First time you asked me out.' I stare at my clown feet, the miracle pills not enough to take the sting off that awful memory. 'Well. "Asked".'

'Uh, no. No, it wasn't him.' Haruki shuffles awkwardly. 'It was Tom. I'm really sorry about that, by the way. People are jerks.'

'Yeah.' My tone is flat, and I hate myself for it. I don't want Haruki to think I'm some self-loathing downer. But I can't think of anything else to say, and the pause has stretched past awkward all the way into agonizing.

'Okay. Well . . . see you tomorrow.' Haruki does a cute little half-wave. 'Probably early, let's be real. I'm a disgustingly prompt human.'

I chuckle, taking another bite of the cinnamon roll. It is *really* good. 'Me too. The movie starts at eight, so what time should we get there?'

'Two-thirty,' he replies, without missing a beat.

Smiling, I tuck a lock of blond hair behind my ear. 'Perfect.'

He looks up at me through thick black eyelashes and nods. 'Perfect.'

I catch up with Gabriela later. Keiko skipped her final class to hitch a ride into the city for a gig, so it's just the two of us strolling out into the Friday afternoon sun, the air of weekend freedom all around.

'Hey, so . . . question. Would you be up for a double date with me and Haruki?' I ask her. 'I know it's kind of awkward. Keiko would be . . . not happy. But it could be really fun.' Although I was initially unsure, I'm now really into the idea. Double dating with my friends and their partners was something I always fantasized about when I longed for a relationship: going bowling, taking road trips to the beach.

Gabriela immediately trips over the front of her flip-flop and has to throw her arms out to prevent herself from hitting the deck. She is adorably clumsy, like the female love interest in rom-coms where the writer clearly has to give her a flaw but doesn't want it to be anything a man could feasibly find repulsive. She blinks and picks up the notepad she dropped. 'Of course! That sounds awesome.'

'Awesome,' I say, arms straining around the stack of textbooks I need for my weekend assignments. Some of Gabriela's friends from the cheer squad pass us as we leave campus and wave at her – then shoot me a weird look, like they don't know whether to be annoyed by me or fascinated by me. After Armawooden, I don't blame them. (Damn it. Don't tell Keiko I'm using her joke.)

Gabriela bites down on the bottom of her lip. 'But . . . yeah. Keiko. Won't she be pissed?'

It's true. She probably will be. And yet that very fact grates on me. Gabriela would do – or *not* do – anything for anyone. She shouldn't have to feel like crap for doing something she wants to do.

With an assuredness I don't truly I feel, I simply shrug and say. 'Let her be.'

12

I don't know if Haruki is actually serious about meeting at two-thirty, but I decide to stroll into town for then anyway. I figure if he was just kidding, I'll drop my resumé around a few places then head to Barnes & Noble and set myself up in the science section with a vanilla latte and the fattest K.C. Cole book I can find.

As it happens, though, Haruki is precisely as big of a nerd as I am. When I pick up my vanilla latte, I find him perched in the B&N coffee shop with *A Brief History Of Time* propped up against his backpack.

He sees me walking over to him, and his face collapses into the most adorable grin. 'Busted.'

I laugh. 'Busted?'

He gestures to the book. 'Doing my homework.'

Frowning, I ditch my purse on the spare seat and lay my coffee cup down on the table. 'I don't remember Torres setting any reading assignments.'

'Not for Torres,' Haruki says. 'For you. The date. You're so smart. It's kind of intimidating.'

I take a seat opposite him, tilting my chin down to mask the absurd grin spreading across my cheeks. 'You're smart too.'

'Not in the way you are.'

'What do you mean?'

He shrugs. 'Like in Physics . . . I learn the concepts, learn the equations, all that. I learn the science, but I don't think I ever truly *understand* it. I can't even think about string theory without my brain dissolving into a puddle of goo.'

I take a slurp of delicious vanilla latte. 'Okay firstly, you using the word "goo" is adorable for reasons I cannot begin to explain.' It feels weird to talk so brazenly and honestly about finding him adorable, but the pills make me feel invincible. I know he's going to be into me no matter what I say. 'Secondly . . . it's supposed to be mind-bending.'

'I guess.' He stares at his empty espresso cup. This is obviously a real source of insecurity for him, and I sympathize. Although I've never doubted my brain, I feel this way about my appearance all the time.

'The thing is, other dimensions are impossible to perceive because we don't experience them.' My hands gesticulate wildly like they always do when someone lets me talk about physics. I picked up the habit from Vati, who has on several occasions given Dad a concussion. 'Like, imagine you were a fish living in a pond. All you know of sunlight is the way it cuts through the water, dim and refracted. So you go about your life convinced that this is just . . . how sunlight is. Because that's the only way you've experienced it. And yet mere meters above you, there's a world where the sun shines differently. How could the fish possibly perceive that world?'

'Yeah.' He nods. 'Yeah, I get it.'

'That's impressive. Because string theory eludes me sometimes too. It hovers at the periphery of my mind, and if I look around too fast it disappears. I have to sneak up on it if I have any hope of understanding it.'

Haruki smiles, running his forefinger around the rim of his cup. For some reason, this causes a flutter deep in my belly. 'I'm glad it's not just me.'

'Of course it's not,' I say, swallowing the situationally inappropriate pang of arousal. 'Look, our brains – and bodies – have been conditioned to see the universe in a certain way. We innately understand the laws of physics because we must abide by them. There's no escaping gravity, for example. We accept it as truth. But have you ever had a dream where you can fly?'

'Yes! I'm always so disappointed to wake up.'

'Oh, it's devastating. But my point is that your brain *can* perceive this dimension where gravity doesn't exist. Somewhere deep in your consciousness, these permutations of our universe exist. And you can access them subconsciously, without even *trying* to wrap your head around it.'

'That's true.' His eyes widen, like he's never thought of it this way before. 'When you're in the dream, you just accept it as fact.'

'Exactly. It's only when we're awake that we're bound by the confines of the dimensions we experience.'

He laughs and rubs his hands over his face. 'You make my head hurt.'

I snort in a super hot way. 'In a good way though, right?'

'The best way.' He leans forward and studies my face in an adoring way. Which feels nice, but also . . . not real. I shake away the discomfort. 'Why do you love this stuff so much?'

My gaze drops. 'I'm not sure you want to open that can of wormholes.'

Haruki shrugs. 'Why not?'

'It's . . . pretty deep. I've never told anyone before.'

'You don't have to share. But I'd like to hear it.'

I begin furiously shredding a pack of sugar between my fingers. It's true, I've never told anyone this before, and I don't think I've ever wanted to. It's always been the small kernel of truth I orbit around. The gravitational field that centers me. Showing it to another person would feel like carving into my chest to show them my inner workings: the flesh and bone and organs that keep me alive.

And yet right here, right now, the idea of opening up to Haruki feels . . . safe. Because I know he's not going to see my inner workings and reject them. The pills make sure of that.

What do I have to lose? Maybe it'll feel good to open up. Maybe it'll even deepen his attraction toward me.

'Okay, so . . . I was adopted, right?' I start, voice a little trembly. 'When I was really small. And I don't have any conscious memories of who I was before then, or what my life was like. Yet I have this recurring dream. I'm in a house — a house I know intimately — and I'm alone.' I don't mention the body. It seems too dark. 'It doesn't feel like . . . just a dream. It's so vivid. When I was younger and first learning about theoretical physics, I was convinced I was accessing the fifth dimension.'

Haruki frowns. 'The fifth dimension?'

Bless his heart. He really doesn't understand string theory. 'Oh, so that's the one where you'd be able to move forward or backward in time. As easily as swimming through a lake or walking down a corridor.'

'Awesome. So you think you're accessing that dimension while you're asleep, and travelling back in time?'

'Not anymore. It's just a memory, albeit a very rich one.'

He scratches the side of his head. 'How do you *know* it's not the fifth dimension?'

'Because I've never moved forward in time,' I explain.

'Unless the whole flying thing is a prophecy.'

Haruki chuckles. 'Here's hoping.'

'Yup.' I take a deep breath, ready to cut my metaphorical chest open. 'So, when I was younger and first learning about string theory, I kept thinking that . . . if I could subconsciously access the fifth dimension, why couldn't I access the others? The sixth dimension, for example. That's where you could see all possible futures, presents, and pasts in universes with the same start conditions as ours.'

'The Big Bang?'

'Exactly. If I could get there, to the sixth dimension, and I could move along those timelines like I can my own . . . I could essentially live two lives. The one I have now, with my dads and my brother and Sirius. And the one . . . the one where I still have my birth mom. Best of both worlds.'

The words settle between us like dust. No, not dust. Something heavier.

The silence isn't uncomfortable, though. Haruki just looks like he's processing the magnitude of what I've just shared. Peeling back the layers of my words to get to the emotional core.

Softly, he asks, 'Do you think about her? Your mom?'

I consider this. I want to make sure my answer is truthful, because everything up until this point has been. And I never get the chance to deep-dive into my brain like this – at least, not with another human being.

'Only in an interdimensional sense,' I say slowly. 'I think it'd be too painful any other way.'

Haruki nods. 'Okay. Hypothetical question. Say the Large Hadron Collider *did* find evidence of these other dimensions, and anyone could access them. Would you?'

'Of course. In a heartbeat. Wouldn't you?'

He chews his lip, thinking hard. 'No. I think it'd destroy all appreciation for what we have now, in these four dimensions. It'd be so easy to get lost in all those permutations of what could have been, what could be in the future. You wouldn't appreciate the right-now. Which is us, sitting in this bookstore, discussing impossible things.' He smiles. 'And it's pretty damn nice.'

I smile back, despite the fact that these things aren't impossible at all. Because I think I see something shift in his eyes; something in the way he sees me. And I don't think it has anything to do with the drugs. It's like he knew I was smart, but now he's peeling back a layer and understanding why, and he actually likes what he finds under there. It feels warm and surreal, and I want more. I buzz with the possibility of it.

Over vanilla lattes and espressos, we spend the next few hours getting to know each other a little better. We talk about his fascination with marine biology, about how his parents were barely around when he was a kid so he's super close with his cousins. His eyes glinting in the industrial-style lighting, we chat about HEMA a little more, and the comic bookstore I used to work at. We debate Marvel versus DC, the best starter Pokémon in the original games (I'm team Bulbasaur, he's team Charmander), and cheesy mid-noughties rom-coms, with which he is surprisingly *au fait*.

At one point, we even read together in near silence, occasionally reading interesting stuff aloud to each other. Not for the first time lately, I feel old and young all at once.

It's impossible in its perfection, this moment. It's the flawless date you see in movies, not real life. As a result, I don't trust it, but I try to enjoy it as best I can.

At seven, we meet Gabriela and Ryan at the diner to grab a pre-movie burger. Gabriela has gone hard on the makeup look – metallic eyes with a feline flick of eyeliner, fluffy brows, nude matte lips, and perfect contouring on her already killer cheekbones. She looks amazing, and it must've taken her hours. She's topped off the look with a plain black sweater, tight skinny jeans and her trusty Birkenstocks. It's petty, but I feel a twist of envy. Gabriela doesn't need miracle pills to get guys' attention. I shake off the ugly emotion as best I can.

Ryan, on the other hand, is wearing the same T-shirt as yesterday and jean shorts. He lets Gabriela slide into the booth first because she likes the window seat: a small, sweet gesture, showing how comfortable they are together, how well they know each other.

I can't wait to get to that point with Haruki, says an excited voice in the back of my head. But the second my subconscious thinks it, I shudder the idea away. It feels presumptuous, like a jinx, entirely at odds with how this is all too good to be true.

We all order shakes – Haruki plumps for vanilla, yaaaasssss – and the pink-haired hostess hands us menus.

As I peruse the sandwich offerings, I feel Ryan's eyes burning into me. At first I think I have something on my face, but then I remember the pills. My heart sinks. I did not think this through.

I remember Gabriela's small voice after Armawooden. '*Sorry, Caro. I want to know too. Ryan was like . . . looking at you funny.*'

Oh god. Am I about to screw up the most stable relationship in history?

Gabriela clears her throat and says, in her soft, feminine voice, 'So Haruki, how's cross-country going? Ryan said you're shooting for a college scholarship?'

I look up, and Haruki is just kind of . . . gazing at me. While before, when it was just the two of us, his attention felt nice, now it's a little sickly and stifling. He doesn't even turn to face Gabs, just mutters, 'What? Um, yeah. Running's great, thanks.'

Gabriela flinches so subtly that only a best friend could catch it – she's such an introvert that making conversation is physically painful for her – but she recovers fast. 'Cool. What's your favorite distance?'

Haruki shrugs. 'Just the standard three-point-one.'

Ryan snorts. 'I still kick his ass every time.' For some reason, he's making his voice deeper than usual.

'Whatever, dude.' Haruki grunts and squares his shoulders cockily. 'I could run for days. You're all speed, no endurance.'

'I endure your company on a daily basis, asshole.'

For god's sake. I roll my eyes at Gabriela, and she smirks quietly into her strawberry-shortcake milkshake. She shares my lack of interest in male feces-flinging contests, but I can tell she's feeling a little wounded after Haruki's brush-offs.

Besides, her long-term boyfriend is currently staring at me, or competing with Haruki to see who can piss the loudest, or whatever it is boys care about when they're together. No wonder she feels uneasy.

I try to get the focus back on to her. 'So Ryan, how cool is it that Gabs hit twenty-two k on her beauty Insta?' Gabriela glows sweetly at the compliment.

He screws his face up. 'Blergh. Girl shit.'

What the hell? He's normally super-supportive of her, always sharing her posts to his story with sweet comments. Is he trying to put down 'girl shit' because he doesn't think that's something I'm into?

'Yeah,' Haruki agrees. 'Not for me.'

This conversation is souring fast.

Gabriela's shoulders visibly drop. Through gritted teeth, I say firmly, 'Well, I think it's awesome.'

There's an awkward silence. We all drink our milkshakes, and Ryan stares at me some more. Not with annoyance at my snark, I don't think, but with lust. It feels strange to believe that to be the reason, but there's something in the magnetic quality of his gaze. Gabriela looks sideways at him. Guilt squeezes my guts. I hate it, I hate it, I hate it.

Haruki is the first to break the quiet. 'So what movie are we seeing?'

'That new rom-com with Rebel Wilson,' I say, trying to keep the edge out of my voice. I'm still irritated at the way they just took a dump on Gabriela's passion. 'It's supposed to be awesome. I've been watching the press junkets on YouTube for weeks.'

'Really?' Ryan asks. 'But you're so smart. I wouldn't think you'd be into girly rom-com nonsense.' By the weirdly flirtatious look on his face, I can tell he's stupid enough to think he's complimenting me.

I feel Haruki tense next to me, but again, he says nothing to my defense. Guys are so spineless sometimes. But then I think of the way Gabriela and I tiptoe around Keiko, and I realize standing up to your friends just isn't that easy, irrespective of genitalia.

But Ryan isn't my friend. And even though I hate conflict, I can't stand it when people are dicks to my pals. Especially Gabriela, who'd never speak up for herself. So I fold my arms and say, 'Unfortunately, your IQ is not high enough to understand why that's such an ignorant statement.'

Gabriela looks at me pleadingly. 'Caro, don't . . .'

'No, it's cool.' Ryan leans back in his chair and runs his eyes up and down me appraisingly in a way that makes me shudder. 'She's feisty. I like that.'

'Dude,' Haruki finally says. My knight in shining armour. (You can't see my face right now, but that's sarcasm.)

Gabriela's perfectly painted face drops, and I know she's seconds away from crying. Her eyes are bright and shiny, and her bottom lip trembles as she says, 'I'm leaving.'

Within seconds, she's grabbed her purse, clambered awkwardly over Ryan, who's too busy staring at me to let her out, and stormed toward the exit.

'Let me out,' I say to Haruki, who has the aisle seat. 'I'm leaving too.'

'But you really wanted to see this movie,' Haruki says half-heartedly. 'Please, stay.'

'I said I'm leaving,' I insist, standing up and draining the rest of my milkshake because I might be upset but I'm not a shake-waster, damnit.

'Okay,' Haruki mumbles, reluctantly letting me out of the booth. 'I'll see you at school?'

To the horror of my past self, I don't reply. I stride away after Gabriela, out on to the warm street. The sun is low in the sky and blinds me as I look up and down the road, hoping for a glimpse of shiny brown hair and silver eyes, but I'm too late. She's gone.

On my walk home, I try calling and texting her dozens of times, but nope. She's ghosting me. Usually when one of us goes all Nearly Headless Nick, we'll send ghost emojis until they finally relent, but I can't bring myself to do that. Because yeah, Ryan is clearly the dick here. And Haruki, too. But deep down, it's mainly my fault.

My little miracle drugs caused this whole mess and hurt my sweet friend in the process. There's a hollow pit of guilt sitting in my stomach like an avocado stone.

If I keep taking these pheromones, is this how it's going to be? Alright, so Ryan was an asshole tonight, but he's usually so kind and caring with Gabriela. Am I going to ruin that? Am I going to devastate my best friend over and over again?

Hell, am I going to ruin relationships everywhere I go?

I mean . . . people are often attracted to other people even when they're in a relationship. You can still appreciate someone's beauty even if you have a romantic partner. It's when you act on it that it's a problem. Hot people can't be held accountable for their own hotness, right? Keiko doesn't let herself get bogged down in whether her hotness causes other people's relationships to fail. She just embraces her striking looks and lets other people deal with the consequences. Still, the look of quiet devastation on Gabriela's face tonight rocked me.

I should stop taking the drugs. I should. I *should*.

And yet I imagine going back to my normal life, where Haruki doesn't like me and people look straight through me, where my future is all science and no love, and I just . . . I can't. The thought is a clamp around my heart. I feel so close to where I want to be with Haruki. It's within touching distance. And I don't know if I can let it go.

I know that makes me weak. I know it makes me selfish. I hate myself for it, and yet love is a drug I'm becoming quickly hooked on.

My phone dings with a group-chat notification, and I open it faster than the speed of light, but it's not Gabs. It's Keiko.

Ya gurl has a pussy problem. Pls bring me UTI meds asap. I'm pissing pure magma???

Then:

Caro, you said you wanted a Pompeii exhibit. WELL.

I laugh at first, but my guilt intensifies. We didn't tell her we were hanging out without her tonight, and when that comes to light, there's going to be another fallout on my hands.

Might as well rip off the Band-Aid. I open up the private message between me and Keiko and say:

Coming over now. I'll swing by the pharmacy on my way.

We hang out in Keiko's bathroom until the meds kick in. She perches on the toilet, plaid pyjama bottoms hanging around her ankles, while I sit with my back against the door, forming a barricade. The lock has been broken since forever, and the last thing we want is Momo parading in and asking when Keiko became part-volcano.

'So then my mom was like, Keiko, you need to dye your hair back to normal. The blue is really upsetting your grandma.' Right now, her sleek blue locks are pulled up in a messy bun, undercut on full display. 'And then I was like, bitch, grandma's gonna be blue soon enough anyway.'

'Why?' I ask innocently. 'Is she part Smurf?'

'She's gonna die.' Keiko taps her temple with her forefinger. 'Aren't you supposed to be smart?'

'And that doesn't bother you? That she's gonna die?'

'I mean. It does. I'm not a monster. But she's been on my back for years about my appearance. By the look on her face when she saw the undercut, you'd think I'd broken into her house and bleached her asshole while she slept.'

I snort. Keiko always goes all-in on the vulgarity when Gabriela isn't here to wince about it.

Gabriela. My stomach clenches. I check my phone: nothing. Well, not nothing. There's a selfie of Vati deep-throating a parsnip. Honestly, I'm going to ring child services any day now.

'Kiks,' I say slowly, still staring at my phone. 'I have something to tell you.'

'Oh my god, are you dying? I'm so sorry for being so insensitive about blue people. I'll make sure the person who does your corpse's makeup covers up the cerulean tinge. Wait, that's what Gabs could do! Makeup for dead people! Why should death stop you from rocking a statement lip?'

'Actually, it's about Gabriela.' I swallow hard, mouth suddenly dry. 'We went on a double date tonight. With Haruki and Ryan.'

'Oh.' The word is short and heavy.

'It . . . didn't end well.' I tap my phone screen with the nail on my index finger; a nervous tic. 'We were going to see a movie, but it didn't even get that far. Ryan was being a jerk, and he wouldn't stop staring at me, so Gabs stormed off.

Now she won't answer her phone.'

Keiko nods and starts peeing again. 'That sucks.'

'Yeah.' Neither of us say anything for a few beats. 'I think I took the eggplant thing too far.'

She flushes the loo, pulls her pants up and washes her hands with jojoba soap. 'What?'

'With the staring. Honestly, Ryan was looking at me like I was a Jenner sister. I feel kind of bad for doing that . . . spell, or whatever. I ruined Gabriela's date.'

To my enormous surprise, Keiko actually cackles with laughter. 'I don't know how to tell you this, Caro, but eggplant magic isn't real. If Ryan was staring at you, there's another reason.'

I frown. 'Like what?'

She takes a seat on the floor, leaning back against the bathtub. 'You really don't consider yourself attractive, do you?'

'Well, no. Obviously.'

Keiko sighs and rolls her eyes. 'Why is that obvious?'

I stare at her like she's a moron. 'Because of the way I look.'

'You're kidding me, right?'

'No? I mean. We all know it's a thing. I'm not pretty.' I think of when they were trying to console me during cross-country, when Haruki had ignored me. They showered me in compliments, but none were about my looks. 'And that's fine,' I add, even though it's not and it hurts. 'I have

146

my brain. But that doesn't explain why Ryan was staring at me. He wouldn't know a subatomic particle if it kicked him in the dick.'

Keiko shakes her head vigorously, the messy blue top-knot waggling all over the place. 'Back the fuck up. You're not pretty? Are you kidding? Caro. You're beautiful.'

'No, I'm not.'

'I can't tell if you're trolling me. Do you honestly *not* see that you're beautiful?'

At first I think she's blowing smoke up my ass just because I've directly addressed the issue. But instead of staring at the ground, gritting her teeth through the uncomfortable lie, she's looking at me intensely.

'I'm *not*,' I argue. 'Not like you or Gabriela.'

She shrugs as though this statement is meaningless. 'Yeah, I mean, we all look different. But we're all beautiful, too. You've got that distinctive fifties movie-star thing going on.'

'I guess . . .'

'No, listen. There are so many different types of beautiful. Sunsets and fairy lights and peonies and mountains and ballgowns . . . none of them look even remotely alike, but they're all undeniably beautiful. That's like us.' She studies my face, smiling. 'I think you're like . . . a lake on a winter morning.'

God, it's so ridiculous, but I actually tear up with the shock of it. In the past, whenever I've shown signs of low self esteem, they give me the talk on how beauty doesn't matter, about how nobody has the obligation to be pretty. And it's true. But I guess it's just human nature to want what you don't have.

And now, this. From Keiko, the most beautiful person in the world.

'Nobody's ever said that to me before,' I mumble. Instead of tapping my phone, I clutch it tightly. 'About being beautiful. Well, apart from Vati. But he is legally bound to say such things.'

Keiko shuffles over to me on her knees and cups my face in her hands. They smell of jojoba and almond oil. 'Caro, listen to me.' Her eyes flicker back and forward across my face, like she's reading a book. 'You're beautiful. I don't want you to ever think otherwise, okay?'

'Okay,' I say, and it just means so fucking much. Because somehow I know she's not bullshitting me. I can feel it in the heat of her gaze.

And yet. And yet, and yet, and yet.

The pills.

Is she just . . . Is she only saying these things because of the pheromones? The thought crushes me.

She pulls her hands away, and the air around my face feels cool without them.

'So, you're not mad?' I ask, dabbing my eyes on the back of my sleeve.

Pushing a cuticle down with her thumbnail, she says, 'About what?'

'Me and Gabriela going on the double date. And not telling you.'

'No,' she says, jaw taut. 'Of course not.'

'Keiko . . .'

'I'm not mad,' she insists, cutting me off. 'God, my vagina is ablaze.'

'Are you sure?'

'Yes. You could fry bacon down there.'

'I mean about not being mad.'

'I'm sure.' She goes to suck her thumb, like she did when she was a kid, but stops herself just in time, sucking on her bottom lip instead. She looks kind of sad, even if she isn't angry. 'But just . . . tell me next time, okay? It's okay to hang out without me. I just don't like feeling like you're doing it behind my back. That's when a bitch gets paranoid.'

I smile. 'Deal.'

Keiko and I met back in kindergarten. I can barely remember those early days, but Vati says I had to be dragged there on my first day kicking and screaming in my tiny overalls. I was an anxious kid. There was the trauma of being torn away from my birth mother, the trauma of being told I had two new parents and both were men and I had to forget the notion of a mother altogether. The trauma of overcoming that trauma and creating a happy little nest with the two overgrown weirdos who'd taken me in, only to be told that actually, I had to spend hours and hours every day *away* from that nest I'd grown to love so much.

So I arrived at kindergarten a blubbery, snotty mess, and set myself up in a quiet corner arranging the building blocks by colour and size. For the first few weeks, I wouldn't speak to anyone, wouldn't participate in the group activities, and cried whenever anyone tried to hold me. I was swiftly assessed for autism, which came back inconclusive. It must've been pretty difficult for any child psychologist to try to untangle that web, but the eventual verdict was that my symptoms were of PTSD, not ASD.

Meanwhile, Keiko had already established herself as queen of the beehive. She wore glittery scrunchies and jelly shoes and her mom let her paint her nails blue, so she had an army of fans and a whole bunch of teachers infatuated with her cuteness.

A few weeks in, I was robotically arranging my building blocks when Keiko came over and picked one up. I immediately started crying, but instead of freaking out or walking away, Keiko sat cross-legged next to me, wrapped her pudgy little arms around my shoulders, and told me it was going to be okay. I sobbed and sniffled. She asked me what I was building, and I said I was just arranging things. She said that was okay, and that maybe we could make a castle where every tower was a block of the same colour. That way things could still be arranged, but we'd also have a cool castle to play with.

Of course, this charming tale has been recounted by Vati, who had it recounted to him by a teacher, but it honestly hasn't been embellished in the thirteen years since it happened. And it just . . . rings true. I can't remember it, as such, but it feels right.

From then on, we were inseparable. Keiko's army of fans was jealous of me, but Keiko didn't care. She liked me most. That continued throughout grade school, and kids were often mean about me, saying that Keiko should ditch me and hang out with the Populars. But she never did. And she told them precisely where to shove it.

So the way I see it is that . . . so what if she's a little possessive? For the longest time, I've been hers and she's been mine. Even if I've never really understood why she liked me to begin with.

13

When I get home, I don't take the pills straight away. I'm not going to see Haruki or any other eligible bachelors tomorrow, so I give my body – and my conscience – a day off.

On Sunday morning, I lie in bed for much longer than I usually do, drinking milky coffee and playing Words With Friends against Leo, who prefers to communicate with me through the medium of board games as opposed to actual human conversation. My window is cranked open to let some fresh air in, and Vati can be heard cutting the grass while belting out the Pina Colada song at the top of his lungs. Every time he croons about making love at midnight, a small piece of me dies.

For some reason, as I try to figure out what word I can possibly play with the letters QVBNNTX, I keep running over last night in my head. Not the disastrous date, but the moment with Keiko on her bathroom floor. Her hands cupping my face as she told me I'm beautiful. I'm not sure why it means so much, hearing those words from her. I'm not sure why she said it so passionately, like she really, desperately wanted me to believe it.

Maybe it means so much because I can't remember her ever saying it to me before. Maybe she said it so passionately because she was only just realizing it for the first time. I don't know. Whatever the reason, I want to relive that moment over and over again, savoring every detail. I want to bask in its warmth.

And I want to know that it wasn't because of the pills. But how can I?

On Sunday night, Gabriela eventually starts messaging back as though nothing has happened. When I message her separately to ask if she's okay, she just writes *yep, why wouldn't i be?* and even though I'm dying to ask whether she and Ryan are okay, I take her tone as my cue to leave it alone until she wants to talk about it. Even though I'm glad we're still okay, my stomach still behaves largely like a tumble dryer. Guilt is the worst emotion, don't @ me.

Keiko's continuous stream of commentary does ease the pain, somewhat.

Okay: Fuck, Marry, Kill. Nicki Minaj, Cardi B, Iggy Azalea. Go.

Two seconds later:

I literally don't care that you're not lesbians. You gotta fuck one. Don't be homophobes.

Then:

Also there's only one correct combination, so choose your next words carefully. Or you'll meet the same fate as Momo's unicorn collection. #MassHornAmputation

I consider this cautiously, trying to figure out not just who I would fuck, marry or kill, but who Keiko would too. I fire off the combination I think is correct.

Ding, ding, ding! We have a winner! Caro Kerber-Murphy, your horn remains intact another day.

I snort and type a response.

This is a really fucked up gameshow. I'm totally reporting you to the Federal Communications Commission.

Gabriela doesn't really contribute, but there's nothing new there. Sometimes I wonder if she finds the nonsense conversations Keiko and I have annoying. I'm pretty sure her cheerleader friends don't make jokes about unicorn mutilation.

Haruki and I don't have each other's numbers, and for a while I don't even open the Instagram app to see if I have a message from him. Okay, so he technically didn't do anything wrong, apart from maybe being a coward in the face of a douchebag friend. And transform into a different human being the second his guy pal showed up. But apart from that, we had an awesome afternoon in B&N. Still, something has soured after last night.

It's weird. Past me would've done anything just to talk to Haruki, and now I'm reluctant even to open the app and see if he's tried to reach out. I think of the me of a few weeks ago, lying in bed and willing my phone to buzz with something, *anything* to prove I'm not a pariah. That me would've shit herself there and then if Haruki had got in touch to say *hi, I want to see more of you*. That me would've done anything for it.

Hell, she *did* do anything for it.

When I open Instagram, though, there's no message from Haruki. There are a bunch of new follow requests – almost half from other girls, no doubt trying to see what all the hoohah is about – and I accept them all, glowing a little as I do. There are a million DMs from my group with Keiko and

Gabriela, Keiko having sent us about ten memes in a row.

Keiko has also sent me a video about time crystals, a new state of matter proven to exist alongside solid, liquid and gaseous states. Created in the lab, time crystals are structures that repeat periodically in time rather than space, potentially defying the laws of physics. Keiko has sent me the link with the comment: *wHaT tHe AcTuAl FuCk? How do you understand this shit, my head hurts. Please explain it to me sometime?*

But there's nothing from Haruki.

That's when I realize I *do* care whether or not he talks to me. The lack of communication stings. I want this to be on my terms. I want to be the one calling the shots. I've had a taste of that already, and it's intoxicating. I want more of that feeling – the feeling of being able to do whatever you want without fear or rejection.

The fact is, Haruki is not that interested in me when I'm not around. Apart from the fake-out text Ryan sent from his account, he never messages or calls. There's no point in lying to myself; it's because of the pills. When I'm near him, he can't resist my boosted pheromones. When I'm not around, though, does he wonder what he's doing? Does he think, wait, why did I want to go on that date again? Does he study my selfies and think . . . yikes?

The sensation of powerlessness, of losing control over the situation, makes me feel cold and panicked. Haruki's attraction to me is a fragile thing, at least until we spend enough time together for the connection to take root. I have to let it get that far. I have to give him the time and space to develop real feelings for me.

I pop a pill before I can talk myself out of it; before I can remind myself of the heartbroken look on Gabriela's face when Ryan gazed at me instead of her.

Maybe it's because I talked so candidly about my mom with Haruki in the bookstore, but I have the dream two nights in a row. Something's different, though. I don't wake in a cold sweat, scared out of my mind. The fear is lessened, somehow, as though discussing it head-on has removed some of its hold over me. Instead what I'm left with is a burning, scientific curiosity. A churning desire to know more. What happened? Who am I, really? What would that sixth dimension with my mom look like?

But I can't, I can't, I can't. I can't hurt my dads like that.

On Monday morning, I arrive at school to find Keiko already hanging by my locker. This is a miracle on par with the creation of all things, since she's usually at least an hour late to school. Dressed in a lime green sweater and ankle boots so high they must be giving her vertigo, she looks wide awake, waggling a Tupperware box.

'I made brownies!' she says by way of greeting, opening

the box and wafting the smell of cocoa and sugar in my direction.

'Ohmygod, they smell insane,' I say, digging my hand into the box. Which is . . . a mistake. Since the brownies are . . . sticky. Very sticky.

'Yeah, I don't think I baked them long enough,' Keiko laughs, stifling a yawn with the back of her hand. 'I got impatient and wanted to taste them. They're pretty good, if raw brownie batter is your thing.'

'It just so happens that raw brownie batter is precisely my thing. Do you have a spoon?'

Without hesitation, Keiko whips two spoons out of her black jeans pocket, and we dig in. Give her her due, it is precisely like eating raw brownie batter, in the best way possible. By the time Haruki arrives with my morning cinnamon roll, I'm too stuffed to eat another thing. I stuff it in my locker when he's not looking, and I swear there's the slightest trace of triumph on Keiko's cocoa-smeared face.

Monday is also cross-country day, and the fierce heat is finally losing its edge. There's a breeze on the air, and fine hazy clouds in the sky. Mr Chikomborero, our gym teacher, is hyped. He gives us this overblown speech about how the gods are shining on us today with this dry warmth, and we owe it to them to run our hearts out. Or something. Keiko rolls her eyes so hard that ground tremors can probably be felt in Jakarta.

We set off, and to begin with we fall into our usual pace, which is somewhere between 'snail chasing a leaf' and 'toddler crawling for the first time'. I'm antsy, though, maybe from pent-up guilt, maybe from the intensely sugary brownie batter. I feel myself pulling ahead, pushing my foot too hard on the gas. Keiko and Gabriela struggle to keep up, and no matter how hard I try to rein it in, I can't.

'God, wait up.' Keiko harrumphs. 'What's gotten into you? Have you suddenly transformed into . . . nope, for love nor money I cannot name a single famous sprinter. That is how absurd running is as a concept.'

'Usain Bolt?' I suggest.

'No, I'm not saying bolt. I'm saying stay put.'

Gabriela gulps down some air and breathes out, 'Caro, if you want to run ahead that's cool. Me and Kiks can hang back here.'

'Um, rude, it's not cool.' Keiko comes to a complete stop, hunching over with her palms planted on her thighs. We stop too, even though my legs are tugging me forward. 'We are in this hell together.' A heavy gasp. 'Plus, you hate running as much as we do, right?'

'I dunno,' I shrug, stretching out my calves. 'Maybe I do want to see how fast I can go.'

For a second, Keiko looks like she's been slapped. She

recovers fast, but her features harden regardless. 'Whatever, dude. Your funeral.'

Part of me gets why she's pissed. She's 'hung back' with me ever since kindergarten, going at my pace in social situations, saying no when the Populars continually tried to poach her friendship from me. But I never asked her to do that, and it's not fair of her to hold it over my head now. I've always just accepted it as our dynamic, and yet right now, with the breeze on my face and the yearning ache in my lungs, it's hard not to resent it.

I take off.

My feet thump the dry, compacted earth as I leave the school grounds and emerge into the cool of the woods. Everything stills to a quiet around me; the only things I hear are my sneakers thudding on the ground and my breathing as it steadies into a rhythm. I quickly catch up to the few groups jogging in front of me. Overtaking them sends a jolt of electricity through my veins.

After a mile, when I'm nearly at the halfway point, I've almost caught up with the more serious runners – the ones who don't travel in packs. The ones who see each other as competition, not companions. My lungs are burning now, and lactic acid races up and down my legs. It hurts, but not in a bad way. In an alive way.

The weird thing is, I'm not thinking about science, or

MIT, or Haruki, or Keiko, or the dreams about my mom. I'm putting one foot in front of the other, taking off through the front of my foot like there are springs in my shoes.

I hit halfway and loop back on myself. I still haven't caught the fastest runners, and I was never going to with so much ground to make up – and zero training under my belt – but I'm solidly in the eightieth percentile, ahead of most of my classmates. Every time I think, *Shit, I'm going to have to stop soon before my lungs implode*, I challenge myself to keep going to the next tree, the next rock, the next splintering of sunlight through the canopy.

Half a mile later, I pass Keiko and Gabriela. Gabriela stares at me in amazement, and while I expect Keiko to avert her gaze or tilt her chin upward in defiance, she can't hide the awe in her eyes. They both stop and follow my path back towards the football field.

Now that my friends are watching, I focus all my attention on not dying. My breathing is erratic, my gait out of control, and I know I probably look like an escaped axe murderer, but all I do is push faster, leaning into the pain.

Four hundred meters to go. Three hundred. Two hundred. Final push.

As I cross the finish line, the runners who've already finished gaze at me in astonishment and also horniness. Ryan is there, staring, and my insides cramp with guilt. Mr

Chikomborero looks like he might shit himself from excitement and/or arousal. My blood roars in my ears, but I can just about hear him screaming 'Kerber-Murphy! The gods are within you this day!' and I laugh and collapse to the ground, forehead pressed into the grass.

Fuck. That was fun.

14

All day, the air around me crackles. Guys vie for my attention, sending notes in paper airplanes and offering to carry my lunch to my table in the cafeteria. Haruki comes up to my locker to say hi, to apologize for Ryan's behavior at the weekend, and we plan to hang out after school.

I carefully avoid Ryan himself, which also means I have to avoid Gabriela, ducking into classrooms as they stroll toward me in the hallway, and rejecting their invite to eat at their table at lunch. It sucks, having to hide from my best friend, but it seems like the safest way. I don't want to do any more damage.

Keiko and I end up sitting in the corner of the cafeteria, near Madison Spencer and Guadalupe Martinez, the couple that were kissing in chess club all those weeks ago. Guadalupe is crying softly into Madison's shoulder, and Madison is reassuring her, stroking her hair and squeezing her arm with delicacy and affection. From what I can make out, it sounds like Guadalupe's grandma is sick.

A shiver of self-loathing runs through me, and at first I struggle to figure out why. I am not personally responsible for the terminal illness of an old lady. When I put my finger on it, though, I realize it's because of the shallow lens through which I've been viewing Madison and Guadalupe's relationship. Not bothering to wonder what they're like or what problems they have or why they love each other, but instead fixating on their societal attractiveness and whether it conformed to the Matching Hypothesis. Such a reductive way to view a sweet and caring relationship. Such a reductive way to view the world.

God, what kind of asshole was I? Going around judging everyone in terms of objective hotness? I'm part of the problem. I hated when people judged me for my looks, and I did the exact same thing under the guise of scientific curiosity.

Part of me wants to check in and make sure Madison is okay, but they leave the cafeteria before I pluck up the courage and at chess club they're nowhere to be seen. I beat Mateo for the eleventh time in a row and reject Zane's advances when he offers to fork my queen. (I wish I was joking.) I also play against Nafisa Sharraf, who's on the debate team with Mateo. She's killer at anything to do with strategy and won some kind of Model UN award in our sophomore year. She's an equally impressive chess player, but I actually manage to beat her. She's so stunned by my innovative trapping checkmate with a pawn and a knight that she gives me a literal round of applause. The victory leaves me glowing for hours.

People come up to me in the hallway to compliment me on this morning's random burst of running, and to tell me I should try out for the team. The girls' captain presses her phone number into my hand, in case I want any advice, and no fewer than five guys offer to help me train in the gym. I can only assume this is a euphemism.

While all this is happening, the chip on Keiko's shoulder grows roughly to the size of Honolulu. I can tell that while this was funny and intriguing when it first started happening, and while my roasted honey eggplant spell was as delicious as it was nonsensical, she's getting tired of being overshadowed.

And it makes me anxious. I hate feeling like she's mad at me. She seems to have so much power over me, whether that's making me unspeakably happy with genuine compliments, or giving me tumble-dryer belly because she's pissed.

The outfit she's wearing today is one of her most out there yet: skin-tight purple snakeskin pants, white peplum shirt with huge bell sleeves, and white boots with heels higher than the Empire State. She's dyed her blue hair a delicate lilac, and her undercut is freshly buzzed. Honestly, she looks incredible. The outfit accentuates her soft curves, the heels give her an Amazonian stature, the lipstick pulls your gaze to her pronounced Cupid's bow.

She is trying, hard, to wrangle the attention back from me. But it's not working. And she's becoming a bit of a jerk about it.

'What should I wear to hang out with Haruki tonight?' I ask her as we're leaving school together. Gabs is tutoring, and Keiko has band practice later.

'Doesn't matter, does it?' Keiko stares at her phone as we walk. Like literally not even looking up to see where she's walking. I have no idea how she's not gone all Crash Bandicoot at this point. 'You can get anyone you want no matter what you wear. Overalls or not.'

I mean, this is technically true. Still, the edge in her voice bristles. I decide it's not worth the hassle of calling her out, so I decide to try and lighten the mood instead.

I blink innocently, looking down at my outfit. My legs are already aching from earlier. 'What's wrong with overalls?'

Keiko smirks, but not kindly. 'What's *right* with overalls?'

I hold my hands up. 'Hey, maybe I like looking like a decorator.'

'Each to their own,' she retorts flatly.

Usually I'd just let her sulk in peace, but I don't feel like it today. She's been amazing friend to me over the years, but lately she's been kinda sucky, and I've been a total doormat about it. Maybe I'm still fired up from my running frenzy, because I stop on the sidewalk and wait in place until she does the same. She looks irritated, but not surprised.

'Kiks, what's up?' I ask, keeping my tone level and soft. 'You've been weird with me for weeks now. Just talk to me.'

'I dunno, alright?' She stares into the road, at the line of traffic leaving the school campus. Samira sits behind the wheel of a blue SUV, a sophomore guy with thick black dreads sitting in the passenger seat, playing with her hair. 'Something's changed between us. I don't know what.'

Samira cranks the window down to let some fresh air into the car, and the second she does, her co-pilot cocks his head, then looks out the window at me. Our eyes lock, and he immediately stops playing with Samira's hair. She follows his line of vision, sees me on the sidewalk in my thrifted overalls, and shoots me daggers. Daggers I probably deserve.

I swallow back the guilt and turn to Keiko. 'Is it because I'm getting attention for the first time in . . . well, ever?'

Too fast, she snips, 'It's not that.'

'Well, what is it then?'

A long pause. A gaggle of freshman girls jostle past us as though we're invisible, and I can tell it stings Keiko. She's used to being seen. 'Okay, maybe it's that. I just don't like . . . never mind.'

'What?' I nudge. 'Sharing me?'

'Yes. No. I don't know.'

For a second I consider leaving it be, but I know there's something deeper. I know she's not telling me the whole truth. And who knows when I'll next feel confident enough to stand face-to-face with her and demand she talk. I go straight to the uncomfortable root; the ugly, gnarled thing I suspect is driving this mood of hers.

Another car horn toots appreciatively. We turn around, and it's clear the guy behind the wheel has eyes only for me.

Measuredly, I turn back to Keiko and say, 'You don't like me being the one people look at.'

'God, Caro! No!' she snaps, way more rage in her voice than the situation demands. That's what gives her away. 'Jesus. Nice to know how little you think of me. No benefit of the doubt here.'

My face burns, my anger rising to meet hers. She *is* jealous, and instead of being flattered, I'm pissed. Does our friendship really hinge on me being the unattractive one? On her being my savior; the cool kid who took pity and gathered me under her beautiful wing? Well, fuck it. I'm tired of living in her shadow.

'Whatever, Keiko.' I know that doesn't sound like much, but coming from me, such a dismissal is essentially assault and battery.

I walk home alone, leaving her on the sidewalk amongst a

whole bunch of people who've stopped seeing her and, for better or worse, started seeing me instead.

Having agreed to a sunset stroll, Haruki and I arrange to meet by Gordon at seven. Gordon is the giant elm tree that arcs over the river right where it forks. I have no clue why he's called Gordon. Or whether he's even a he. Is it offensive to gender trees? Whatever. Gordon is definitely a dude.

Haruki is already waiting on a bench by the time I arrive at six-thirty. He leaps up as I walk toward him, arms outstretched. 'You did it!' he yells.

I laugh as I close the distance between us. 'Did what?'

When Haruki wraps his arms around me, I'm surprised. I don't know why, exactly. I've been hugged before, but never in a romantic way. Never intimately. Never by a guy other than my dads.

It doesn't last overly long, just enough for me to sink into his warm arms and inhale his scent – fresh laundry and an expensive, tobacco-y cologne. When he pulls away, I wish it had lasted longer. I pull down my sleeves to hide the goosepimples.

We start walking down the river trail. 'Running,' he explains, and I'd almost forgotten about my question. 'Last time we hung out you said you wanted to give running a go. See how fast you were. How was it?'

I beam. I can't believe he remembered. I can't believe he

paid that much attention to me, to the things I wanted. 'It was so great . . . at the time. My legs are killing me now.'

He looks me up and down and quirks his lip in a gently mocking smile. 'Is that why you're walking like you have a coat hanger up your ass?'

I cackle with laughter. 'Pretty much.'

'Did your friends get mad at you about it, like you thought?'

I'm on the verge of telling him about my blow-up with Keiko, but then I realize the only person I really want to talk to about it right now is . . . Keiko. I want her sassy advice and unwavering confidence that everything will be fine. I want her ability to make me smile and believe in myself. Then I remember that now I *do* believe in myself, she can't handle it. The sadness is hollow and numbing.

Haruki breaks the silence I didn't realize was stretching out. 'I'll take that as a yes. Maybe you need better friends.'

My shoulders tense as I leap to defend them. 'My friends are fucking awesome, thank you. And besides, may I remind you of how Ryan acted last weekend?'

He holds up his hands as though begging for mercy. 'Okay, let's not get into that. I want to enjoy tonight.'

'Fine,' I say, resigning myself to the fact that it's safer not to prompt more questions about *why* Ryan was so fixated on me.

The water gushes alongside us as we walk. It's been azure blue all summer, but today it's a pale, delicate grey. I clear my throat. 'So, tell me about your family. What's it like being . . .'

'Rich?' He says the word as though it's a terminal illness.

'Pretty much,' I reply, even though that's not really what I meant. It *is* interesting that that's how he took it, though. That that's the first word that comes to mind when he thinks of his family.

'Honestly, there's not much I can say that makes me sound like *not* an asshole.' His words have taken on a firmer quality, like he wants this conversation to be on his terms. He's defensive. 'I could say I didn't realize I *was* rich until I went to my grade-school friend's house for the first time, which is true. Or I could say it was pretty great being able to make the coolest HEMA costumes ever, which is also true. Or I could say I feel guilty about it basically all the time, which is . . . also true.'

'Why guilty?' I ask. My parents aren't exactly rich, but they aren't poor either. I don't think about it that much, which I guess makes me privileged as hell.

'My parents aren't good rich people,' he says, playing with the zipper on his black hoodie. 'They don't give to charity or open soup kitchens or even leave all that good a tip when they go out to dinner. They buy handbags and private jets and –'

'You have a private fucking jet?'

He laughs, but stiffly. 'I mean, I'm sure they use it for things other than fucking. But sure.'

'Do you not realize how absurd that is?' I don't know where this judgmental tone comes from, having just had a realisation about my own privilege, but seriously. Who has a private jet in real life?

'Yup. Hence, guilt. A few months ago I read this interview with the Disney heiress, who said that if she was queen of the world, she would pass a law against private jets, because they enable you to get around a certain reality. Like, you don't have to shove your way through an airport terminal, you don't have to interact with other people, you don't have to be patient, you don't have to be uncomfortable. Those are the things that remind us we're human. So, yeah. We're obviously not as rich as the Disneys, but I hate that my parents think they're better than other people just because they have a jet.'

There's a pause as I process this. The vitriol with which he talks about his parents and their worldview is entirely new to me. I can't imagine ever feeling that resentful toward my dads. The thought makes me feel guilty and grateful all at the same time.

'Is there anything you *do* like about them?' I ask tentatively. 'Your parents?'

He considers this, still yanking the zipper up to his throat and then down again. His Adam's apple bobs against it. 'My mom has a killer sense of humor. And my dad . . . I like his brother. My uncle and cousins are so great. They got me into HEMA.'

A middle-aged man is walking a yappy terrier nearby, and the dog is pulling frantically on the lead to try and get to me. I press my lips shut to keep from laughing as the poor man drags his dog in the opposite direction, shooting bemused glances at me, Haruki and Gordon.

By means of explanation, I quickly say, 'He must smell Sirius. Anyway, you keep bringing up HEMA. I like that.'

Some of the tension in his stance softens. 'Maybe because it's a novelty. Gives me kind of a thrill to be able to mention it to a girl and not have her run screaming.'

I make a weird half-laugh, half-*pffft* noise. 'It pays to slum it with the Unpopulars every now and then.'

He stops in his tracks, the same way I did with Keiko earlier, and at first a surge of anxiety courses through me. Is he about to end . . . whatever this is? Did I just break the eggplant spell by reminding him of my social status?

Instead, he takes my hands in his. In that moment, I am so damn grateful for the arrival of fall. No sweat. Nailed it.

My heart flutters as he strokes the backs of my hands with his thumb. 'Hey,' he says. 'Don't do that.'

'Do what?' I ask, my voice breathy and hitching in my throat.

His eyes bore into mine, dark and intense, like he's trying to tell me something of paramount importance. 'Sell yourself short.'

'I mean, it's true,' I say. 'I am unpopular.' Then I grin. 'That doesn't mean I'm not awesome.'

It rocks me to my core to realize I kind of mean it. Is that the pills talking? Or is it a notion that's actually taken root in me? There's no time to unpack it now, in the moment, because:

'Do you mind if I kiss you now?' he asks gently.

Then my breath really *does* catch in my throat. 'Yes. I mean. No. I don't mind. That was a confusingly phrased ques—'

He leans in, all fresh laundry and dimples, and cups my face in his hands. As he presses his lips against mine, I'm both tense and relaxed, happy and scared, a thousand different dichotomies all at once. His lips are soft and taste of Earl Grey tea, and there are no tongues, not like the thirsty style Kevin Cartwright employed. It's sweet and nice, but there's heat underneath it, in the way he presses his muscular body against mine, the way he lightly grazes my bottom lip with his teeth.

I am kissing Haruki Ito. A thousand different past versions of me ache at the thought.

The river babbles in the background. He pulls away, slowly and reluctantly, like the air is treacle.

'Caro . . . will you be my girlfriend?'

There it is. The sentence of my dreams.

I've fantasized about this moment since the second week of freshman year, when Haruki strolled into Math in an overly formal Ralph Lauren button-down and promptly spilled Diet Coke right down the front. His star power was apparent then, because everyone laughed with him, not at him, and multiple kids offered to trade shirts with him. He refused all of them – not because he didn't want a clean shirt, but because he didn't want anyone else to have to wear his dirty one.

From that moment on, I've been infatuated with him. He is kind and hot and smart and universally adored, and I never, never in a million years, thought he would ever be mine.

Now he's finally asking me. And it doesn't feel the way I wanted it to; the way I always thought it would.

Because I cheated. I didn't earn it.

You're being too hard on yourself, a voice in my head insists. People do things to trick other people into finding them attractive all the time. Contoured cheeks and push-up bras and musky perfume. Flattering clothes and hair gel and that Basic Bitch Boy haircut they all have. We're all playing the game, aren't we?

Yet Haruki's question doesn't carry the weight it should. It feels forced and . . . inevitable. It strikes me for the first time that inevitability is not something you want when it comes to romance. The longing, the wondering, the what-ifs are what make these moments so sweet – are what make you truly value another person – and I eliminated all that. I rigged the game, so I knew I was going to win. As a result, this moment feels flat, and I hate that it does.

Haruki's eyes study me intently, his lips full and pink from the kiss.

'Of course I'll be your girlfriend,' I say, and I lean in and kiss him again just so I don't have to force a smile.

15

By the time I get home, my initial discomfort over this turn of events has made way for a level contentment. In open defiance of the Matching Hypothesis, Haruki Ito is my boyfriend. I keep saying those words to myself, over and over again like a mantra.

I am living in a rom-com. This doesn't happen in real life. The hot, charismatic, popular, rich, athletic, smart guy doesn't go for the average-looking dork.

No, I tell myself forcefully. *Not average-looking.* I smile to myself, hitting replay on Keiko's words:

'*Do you honestly not see that you're beautiful? You've got that distinctive fifties movie-star thing going on. I think you're like . . . a lake on a winter morning.*'

The words are precious jewels, for some reason all the more precious because Keiko gifted them to me. I wrap them in tissue and guard them in my heart, not sure whether she'll ever say anything like that again. Whether she'll ever say *anything* to me again. I already regret snapping at her.

The second I'm through the front door, Sirius pins me to the door and begins humping my thigh like it's the last bang of his life. To be fair to him, it might be. This is becoming a nightly ritual: come home from school, endure a thorough leg-boning from my one-eyed hound, then help Dad make dinner. The way all Cinderella stories unfold, right?

Vati is in the living room doing a Zumba DVD completely unironically. I find Dad in the kitchen, chopping carrots for the casserole. I'm horrified to note one of said carrots is the very same cock-and-balls monstrosity that Vati and I found in the garden. I decide there and then to go on hunger strike.

Still, I don't want to break the nightly ritual, so I grab an onion, a knife and a chopping board and start peeling while Dad asks me inane questions about school. Then, while he's off on a diatribe about molarity calculations, I blurt out, 'I have a boyfriend.'

Without missing a beat, Dad asks, 'Has he been recently tested for sexually transmitted infections? It is acceptable to demand paperwork in these situations, Caro. You would be amazed how many individuals feel no qualms in lying about their genital wellbeing.'

'Your obsession with venereal disease is profoundly disturbing,' I mutter. I usually don't mind Dad's matter-of-fact manner. Hell, I love him for it. But I'm starting to wish

I'd told Vati first, enthusiastic madman that he is. 'Is that all you have to say?' I mumble. 'Are you happy for me at least?'

'If you are happy, I am happy.' The way he says it is so heartfelt that my irritation melts away. I squeeze his forearm as he chops next to me, and give him his due, he doesn't flinch at the onion juice I've just smeared all over his sweater.

His words remind me of the conversation I overheard between him and Vati. About how he's going back to work instead of finishing his book just because of me, because he wants to set aside a pot of money for me going to college.

If you are happy, I am happy.

Works both ways, Dad.

Extremely subtly, I clear my throat and say, 'How's the book going?'

His knife slows on the carrot for a moment. 'Actually, I shall be returning to work next week.' He picks up speed again, annihilating Vati's carrot. 'My sabbatical has come to an end, and I am not where I wanted to be with the book.'

I dab my eyes, streaming with hot tears from the son-of-a-bitch onion I'm dicing. I now understand why Vati wears swimming goggles while cooking. 'So take some more time off. Finish it. Get to where you want to be.'

A wistful chuckle. 'Oh, to be young and idealistic. You always were like that.'

'I can't tell if that's a compliment,' I say.

'It is merely a statement. It is up to you to assign value to it.'

He is impossible sometimes. Scraping my onion cubes into a pan with some vegetable oil, I say, 'I still think you should finish your book.'

This time he doesn't even dignify my youthfully naïve statement with a response. 'Will you go and ask Felix to pick some herbs from the garden?'

'Fine.' I leave him to stir the spitting pan and mosey into the living room. 'Vati!' I call over the too-loud salsa music. 'Herbs!'

That's when I realize what he's doing. He's crashed into the coffee table and face-planted the floral lampshade, which he is now wearing like a hat.

'Do you know what I love about Zumba, *Bärchen*?' he wheezes, voice echoing inside the lampshade. 'There are no wrong moves.'

After dinner, I plow through my homework, take a shower, then curl up in my bed to watch *What Happens In Vegas*. Dad is still awake, trying to get as much finished as possible on his book before he returns to work, so I can't sneak downstairs for a cheeky vino lest he immediately drag me to rehab.

As Cameron Diaz and Ashton Kutcher get drunk and irresponsible on my screen, I try to unpack everything that unfolded over the last twenty-four hours. I replay the riverwalk with Haruki in my mind, the soft Earl Grey kiss, the earnest question: *will you be my girlfriend?* But no matter how many times I force myself to recall every single detail, it feels like I'm watching it through a stranger's eyes. Like that was never my story, and I just forced my way into it.

The thing that really keeps prodding at me, though, is my fight with Keiko. I was justified in calling her out, I know I was, but guilt still churns in my stomach. The sight of her standing dejectedly on the sidewalk, a rock in the river of freshmen flowing around her and not even glancing at her wild outfit . . . it makes me sad to my core.

Keiko is my best friend. And my accusations hurt her, no matter how true they were.

You never want to be the person hurting your best friend. You're supposed to be the one protecting them from hurt in the first place. In the last few days, I've done damage to both Gabriela and Keiko, whether directly or indirectly, and it feels awful. I'm normally the safe friend, the steady constant, the emotional support and the provider of awesome science facts. How quickly things change.

The light of the TV screen flickering in my face, I find myself burning to message Keiko. I pick up my phone and put it down again dozens of times, not sure what to write, not sure whether to apologize or not. I don't even necessarily want to talk about the fight. I just want to talk to her. About band practice, the river walk, Vati's collision with the lampshade, Momo's new adventures in mermaid obsession.

Gabriela texts the group chat a picture of the movie night she's having with Ryan, and to ask how it went with Haruki. I tell her we're official now, and she's happy for me. She really is. But it's not the same as Keiko being happy for me. It's terrible to admit, but a friendship trio is never entirely equal. Keiko and I simply have too much history for Gabriela to fully match up. Sweet, earnest Gabriela. It's a betrayal even to think it.

Maybe that's why my relationship with Haruki feels a little flat. I so desperately want Keiko's approval, for her to be happy for me – for her to just be happy, generally – that not having that feels like a key component of this is missing.

Halfway into the movie, I realize I haven't been paying the slightest attention. I turn it off and roll over on to my side in an attempt to fall asleep.

It's useless.

For some reason, I wind up thinking about my dads, and how blessed I am to have them, and how gut-wrenching it was when Keiko lost hers.

She didn't literally lose him, of course. She knew exactly where he was. That was worse, maybe.

We were fourteen, maybe fifteen, that day Keiko called me. Her words were drowned by wracking sobs, and I genuinely, genuinely thought either someone else had died or she was about to do so. My heart ripped out, then, listening to her pain but not understanding it yet, not being able to do anything about it.

'My dad's gone,' she finally choked out.

There it was, I thought. Her dad died. I knew he was out of the country – he often was – and a million awful possibilities flashed through my mind. 'Oh my god. Kiks, I'm sorry. What happened?'

'He's leaving M-mom. Staying in Japan.'

'He's with . . . someone?' I asked. 'Else?'

A fresh wave of tears. 'I don't know. I don't know. Oh g-god, I don't know.'

'I'm coming, Kiks,' I said, kicking my feet into my beat-up Chucks. 'I'm walking over. Stay on the line with me, okay? I'm here. Always, always.'

When I got there, Keiko's mom had gone out with Momo to get ice cream, but Keiko had stayed behind so she could call me. It was me she needed, more than anything.

Late into the night, we talked through it all. She shared memories of him, like he really was dead. She felt about him the way I feel about my dads. A deep, pure love for who he was, and how he made her feel. Until that night, anyway. I distinctly remember wishing I could give her one of mine, or at least share them with her. If I thought it would've taken her pain away, I would've.

We fell asleep hugging on her bed, and I woke up with her hair — still deep brown, back then — in my mouth. She leapt away from me as though I were a carrier of the bubonic plague. From that moment on, we never really talked about her dad again. I tried, but she never wanted to.

When I first heard the news about him, I remember feeling relieved. At least he wasn't dead. This was better. This was easier; survivable. Now I know it was, in many ways, so much worse. If someone dies, you don't feel abandoned, or unloved, or unwanted. You don't feel like you're just not enough to get the people you love to stay with you.

It was around then Keiko started dressing and acting the way she does, always trying to prove herself loveworthy. She got louder, bought new clothes, dyed and shaved her hair. An act of defiance, of desperation. Of needing to be seen.

So, I understand why she is the way she is. I understand why it stings to have the attention she's worked so hard for stolen by her best friend. It's addictive, being seen, being adored, so when it's suddenly taken away or altered, it's like going cold turkey on a drug. No wonder she's acting out. She's in withdrawal.

But I wish she understood that I still see her; have always seen her. Just as she is.

16

Over the next few days, Keiko all but ignores me. No quirky group chat messages, no walking me to chess club, no improvising new song lyrics during lunch. No science articles or YouTube videos she excitedly finds and shares, just because they reminded her of me. No brownie sludge or vagina jokes. My life doesn't really feel like my life without her.

Gabriela is caught in the middle, but I quickly realize that my fierce friendship with Keiko is the glue that holds the trio together. Without that, everything just kind of falls apart. Gabriela doesn't have the sway or conviction to get us talking to each other again, let alone to take the reins and instigate some Fun Times. Part of me thinks she could if she really wanted to, but after a few hours of half-heartedly trying to get us to kiss and make up, she abandons the situation and hangs out with Ryan and her cheerleading friends instead. Maybe she's grateful for the excuse to spend time with them instead of us. No unicorn mutilation jokes in sight.

I guess in a lot of ways, it's simpler like this. The less I see of Gabriela, the less I see of Ryan, and the more their relationship has the chance to mend after the damage I caused on the double date.

I spend most of the time between classes and at lunch with Haruki. Now that we're official, things are escalating quickly – we kiss a lot, everywhere, and he asks when he can meet my dads. I shudder at the thought of Vati forcing poor defenceless Haruki to endure a carroty condom demonstration, but how can you really tell your new boyfriend this? I had hoped Vati's tumble into the lampshade might have knocked some sense into him, but he's more nuts than ever. A veritable cashew of insanity.

Despite the underlying sense of guilt and weirdness, I am genuinely enjoying spending time with Haruki. He's funny and smart and sweet, even if he does turn into your basic jock bro when his friends are around. And he makes me feel so . . . wanted.

It's hard to explain how intoxicating it is to go from a nobody to a somebody. It's hard to really convey how good it feels to walk down the hallway with your head held high, hundreds of eyes on you as though you're a contestant on America's Next Top Model, not some rando physics nerd with a penchant for overalls. (Space-time continuum, but make it fashion.)

The feeling of power, of desirability, is a drug more potent than any pheromone pill.

On Thursday, Haruki and I are eating mac and cheese in the cafeteria. A couple of his track and field friends are sitting with us, including Samira and her new boyfriend, Khalil. He's the guy who practically hung out of his car window panting at me when I was on the sidewalk arguing with Keiko, and he doesn't let up today.

Dressed in a blue tracksuit, Samira isn't trying desperately to get his attention back, instead just flicking through her phone and picking at her pasta. I like that about her. I like Samira a lot, actually, her cool confidence, and I'm not the only one. Keiko sits across the room with Gabriela and the cheerleaders, flicking her jealous gaze over to us whenever she thinks we're not looking.

I wish Samira was gay, I think. So Keiko would have a chance with her. But the thought sends a funny twist of jealousy roiling through my chest.

I hate the idea of her hanging out with Samira instead of me, of having her passionate attention redirected toward someone else. It makes me sick with jealousy. An ugly emotion, but I cannot shake it off no matter how gross I feel.

So this is how Keiko feels about having to share me. Suddenly I get it. Truly get it.

I make a decision, then.

Turning to Haruki, I lower my voice and say, 'Hey, what are you doing this weekend?'

He smiles lazily, crunching down on a carrot stick. He's way more health-focused than most other teenage boys, despite being recently converted to the church of vanilla milkshakes. 'You mean what are we doing.'

'I was hoping you would say that,' I say, as Khalil mimes gagging. Haruki rolls his eyes in return, like, *I know, man, but what can I do?* I ignore it as best I can and push forward with my pitch. 'Keiko has a gig in the city on Saturday night. A small, intimate one, but it's at a venue where big bookers and record-label scouts sometimes hang out. I know she's nervous, and it'd be cool to go support her.'

He frowns. 'I thought you guys weren't talking?'

'We aren't. But she's still my person.'

He prods me playfully with a carrot stick. 'Wait, aren't I your person?'

'Of course,' I say quickly. 'It's just different.'

Unfortunately, Vati volunteers his services as cab driver into the city. I am already mortified by the prospect, but I guess it could be worse. Dad could be ferrying us while simultaneously interrogating Haruki about his venereal history. So I should really count my blessings.

Things don't start too well when Haruki rings my front

doorbell, and Vati places one of the garden gnomes on the inside door mat, opens the door and hides behind it. Then, I shit you not, in a high-pitched voice, he says, 'Greetings, human. Welcome to my humble gnome.'

As he guffaws wildly from his hiding spot, I have to ask: why did child services ever grant custody of me to such an overgrown toddler?

Give Haruki his due, he joins in with the banter as best he can. 'Hello, sir. I have only honorable intentions with your daughter, regardless of my Y chromognomes.'

Vati laughs so hard at this I actually worry he might rupture his spleen.

After that, Haruki comes in to meet Dad over a glass of iced tea. Thankfully Vati refrains from a) cupcake aprons and b) *Mean Girls* references, for which I am eternally grateful. Haruki talks about his aspirations to study marine biology, and eventually go into reef restoration. This makes Dad positively giddy, if he were capable of such a thing. But he does do a funny little skip on his way to the freezer.

Hearing Haruki say he plans to move to Madagascar and save the reefs should rattle me. I'm an overthinker, right? And this throws a spanner in the works of my grand plan for how our life together will unfold. How could I take Volta and Galilei away from their grandfathers? What if Schrödinger hates the heat?

But I find myself apathetic to the idea of my boyfriend (still weird) moving to the other side of the world.

Maybe I'm just nervous. All I can think about is tonight. Not only am I scared Keiko will be pissed at us showing up unannounced, but also I really, really want it to go well for her. What if our presence there throws her off? On a night when it really matters that she's on her game?

But I want to be there. God, I want to be there. It feels like forever since I've heard her husky voice sing about love and heritage and identity. I crave it now, when we're not talking, more than ever. Up until very recently, my life had a constant Keiko soundtrack, and having it suddenly shut off feels like a form of sensory deprivation.

Vowing to stand right at the back, where she won't see me and be distracted, I text Gabriela to make sure she's still up for meeting us outside the venue five minutes before doors open.

oh crap, i lost track of time! been hanging with the cheer squad. you guys go in and i'll get there soon as i can??

The fact this gig isn't as important to her as it is to Keiko – or to me – shouldn't annoy me, but it does. I'm used to being blown off so she can hang out with Ryan, but being blown off in lieu of other friends feels somehow worse.

The drive into the city with Vati is a literal hellride. For one thing, he decides to play the *Pitch Perfect* soundtrack from beginning to end, performing every single acappella part all at once. Weirdly, though, I don't find myself embarrassed or anxious that Haruki will think my family is odd. We *are* odd. That's what makes us great. And deep down, I think that's what Haruki likes about me. I'm not like every other jock he hangs out with. As I watch him actually join in with the tenor parts in the riff-off, I think maybe being around me gives him permission to be his full weird self too.

Traffic is light, so we get to the venue ten minutes before doors, and my heart swells with pride when I see dozens and dozens of people queuing already. A group of sophomores from our school wear matching purple tees with Keiko's first album cover printed on the front, and there's a whole bunch of girls in their late twenties chatting excitedly about the show. There are a few guys, mostly on the arms of their girlfriends, but it's mostly women. Women who feel empowered by Keiko's music.

My cheeks almost split from smiling. Keiko has fans. How fucking cool is that?

Vati stops us as we're climbing out of the car. 'Now, I have some bad news for you. In your iced tea earlier, I put miniscule tracking devices. Almost invisible to the naked eye. So if you break your curfew – well, ladies, the FBI will be after you faster than you can say *Karotteschwanz*.'

Haruki frowns. 'What's —'

'Don't ask,' I say hurriedly, not in any rush to explain. 'Vati, *du machst sich zum Affen.*'

You're making an ape of yourself. A German idiom I learned just for him.

Haruki looks impressed, while Vati is apoplectic with excitement. He thumps the steering wheel with his fist and roars with laughter. '*Bärchen, ich liebe dich!*'

He revs the engine, and we finally escape on to the sidewalk. The windows are down, and as he drives away, I can hear him singing the Austrian national anthem. '*Land der Berge! Land am Strome! La la la la la!*'

Haruki follows the car with his gaze almost . . . wistfully? Remembering his own strained relationship with his absentee dad, I reach out and squeeze his hand. He pecks a light kiss on my cheek, and it's so sweet I can't help but smile.

'Are you excited?' he asks me, our faces close together as we join the end of the line. 'You seem excited.'

'Yeah! And a little nervous, I guess.' It's true. I'm jittery as hell. I have no clue how Keiko does this.

'Why nervous?' Haruki says. He wraps his arms around me, and it's nice, but I'm kind of overheating in the evening warmth.

'I want her to do well,' I say into his chest. 'She's so ready to kick this thing to the next level, and tonight could be the night she makes a real break.'

Haruki frowns and looks up at the sign for the club. There are lights out in the name, and the black paint around it is peeling. 'Really? Here?'

'It's apparently the place a bunch of stars were discovered in the eighties and nineties, and everyone from music journalists to record-label scouts still hang out here on the reg.' I scan the queue for anyone who could be a booker or scout, before realizing they probably don't queue with the cattle. 'It may look small and dingy, but the fact she got booked here is legit awesome.'

Haruki kisses me on the forehead. 'I love the passion you have for your friends.'

By the time the doors open, the line trails down the block and wraps around the corner. The bouncers check our IDs and give us different colored wristbands to those who meet the drinking age, so the bartenders know they can only serve us soft drinks. The club's ethos is that nobody should be excluded from great music just because they're teenagers, and honestly I think that's pretty cool.

The place may look seedy as hell from the outside, but inside it's just laidback and comfortable. The booths have cracked leather seats in deep emerald green, and there are those chic industrial lights hanging over each one. The floor is exposed concrete, and the black walls are covered in black-and-white pictures of all the famous people who've performed here over the years.

Haruki and I grab a booth near the back, away from the stage. Haruki goes up to the bar to get a couple of sodas, and I text Gabriela to let her know where we are. She doesn't reply.

Within minutes, the place is packed out. It's still a half hour until Keiko takes to the stage – she's the supporting act for Jaxon Zentner, the singer-songwriter who's headlining. I've heard his stuff and honestly, he's not as good as Keiko. I'm not just saying that. He sings his lyrics without really feeling them, whereas with Keiko it comes from the soul.

I'm a bundle of nerves, and when Haruki returns with two lemonades, I can barely focus on what he's saying to me. Something about what kind of music he's into, and whether or not I'm a rap girl. I mumble noncommittally, crackling with anticipation for the moment the background music dims, the spotlights crank on and Keiko takes the stage.

For some reason, when it finally happens, I jump a little in my seat. That's how on edge I am. Gabriela still hasn't even replied, let alone arrived.

Keiko's band takes the stage first, and I immediately notice that her drummer, Chris, has abandoned his usual kit and is carrying a huge taiko drum – as are two other girls I've never seen before. In fact, her entire band has multiplied. There are a couple of guys each with a different type of flute, a girl with a bronze gong. Kiera is there with her acoustic guitar, and Jocelyn is on bass, but there's also a lute and a mouthpiece resting on an amp.

What are you up to, Kiks?

They start up, and it's like nothing I've never heard. It's a little like gagaku, a type of ancient Japanese court music Keiko played for me once. But where that was a little screechy, a little coarse, this is something new entirely. It's bouncy and uplifting. The taiko drums make your heart beat faster, and the flutes add a sweetness, but there's still something very Keiko in the quirky guitar riffs. It shouldn't work, but my god, it really does.

Keiko walks on stage to rapturous applause and wolf-whistles from the crowd. Lots of people have abandoned their booths and are standing in the wide open space in front of the stage, but when Haruki asks if I want to do the same, I tell him I want to stay out of sight.

She. Looks. Killer.

She's wearing this buttercup-yellow mini dress with a huge, structured ruffle of fabric snaking from her shoulder to her hip. Her super high shoes are metallic with a block heel and gemstones on the straps, and she wears chunky silver bracelets and giant hoop earrings. Her lilac hair has been curled and backcombed to within an inch of its life, and cascades down her back in lavender waves.

As the taiko drums suddenly die down, the air is thick with anticipation. She leaves it for a perfect beat, just long enough that we're desperate for more, but not long enough that it's getting weird. Then she opens her mouth and launches straight into *Upside Downside*.

Everyone screams like she's literal Beyoncé.

The song has been remixed, reworked, and while it was once your traditionally great rock song, this has style and flair. It feels fresh and new. It's rock mixed with gagaku mixed with something quirkier. Something entirely Keiko.

It goes too fast. I want to listen to it forever.

'Whaddup, Charleston?' she yells. 'How are we doin' tonight?'

The charisma bleeds from her. The cheers and screams wash over her, and I can almost feel her drawing power from it.

The next few songs of the set are other old classics – *Mess You Up, Power of Pretty* – but all reworked in this new style. Her voice is deeper, raunchier, more certain than before. It was always smooth and easy, but there's a fierceness, a forcefulness to it now. It's electric.

She sounds young and old all at once.

As I listen to *Fight Or Flight*, I cannot believe how hard she's been working. Sure, I know she's often busy with band practice, but this? This basically inventing a new genre of music? She must be up all night, every night, mixing and remixing with her headphones on while Momo sleeps in the bed beside her. She is . . . astounding. And yet she still always has time for me.

Suddenly it seems so absurd that I ever thought she was self-absorbed, always talking about her music. She's been creating something groundbreaking. Of course she wanted to talk about it with her fucking best friends. Did I ever really ask any questions, though? Or did I just let her ramble, tuning her out, not fully listening to the fact my best friend is a genius and a pioneer? I've missed out on watching this amazing thing unfold, this thing that might just make musical history, and for what? Because I was too busy chasing boys, and getting annoyed when she didn't ask me enough about it?

I can feel Haruki's gaze on me as I watch her absolutely owning the stage, but I can't tear my eyes away for two seconds to return his look. He scoots closer to me and rests a hand on my thigh, but I barely notice.

The song ends, and Keiko takes a sip of water, then grabs the mic from its stand.

'Are y'all ready to hear something new?' she shouts. The crowd cheers and whistles. 'I know, y'all, I know. You just wanna be able to sing along, right? How can you do that if you don't know the song? But you just gotta trust me on this.

It's called *Bones and Stardust.*'

Jocelyn starts plucking a simple baseline. Chris and the other two taiko drummers kick in with a beat that's somewhere between uplifting and urgent. Then the flutes, and the acoustic guitar. I know I'm not doing it justice, but it's the kind of combination you just want as the backdrop to your entire life. The music you listen to when you want to feel happy, but you also want to get shit done.

Then Keiko starts to sing.

> *Why are you so afraid?*
> *Why are you so afraid of your own reflection*
> *When your reflection is the stars you love*
> *The sky above*
> *Is in you*
> *Why are you so afraid when you are the universe*
> *And the universe is you?*

Everything in me heats up.

I can't explain how I know. It's something in the way she sings the words. Yes, it's in that new, deep, raw style. But it also has the same quality of her voice when it's just me and her, talking about nothing. It's both informal and passionate. It's comfortable and assured. It's laughing about beauty and blazing vaginas on her bathroom floor, her hands around my face, smelling of jojoba almond soap.

It's for me. She's singing about me, and the way I see myself.

Before I've even registered what I'm doing, I'm sliding out of the booth and on to the floor. I push toward the front.

Why are you so afraid?
Why are you so afraid of your own dimensions
When your dimensions are your history
There's eternity
Within you
Why are you so afraid when you are the universe
And the universe is you?

The final bodies part, and then I'm there, I'm a few feet away from her yellow dress and her lilac hair and her fiery eyes.

She spots me right as she's about to launch into the chorus. When our gaze locks, there's a tiny catch in her throat, and I can tell she's missed her cue by a few milliseconds. She lets the band play an extra bar, tugs her eyes away from mine, and lets rip.

You are bones and you are stardust
And you must, you must not betray
Your reflection, your dimensions

Not to mention
The love that burns inside you
Like bones and stardust

By the end of the chorus, her voice is a roar.

Something dormant awakens in me, then. And it's so overwhelming that I cannot even begin to understand it.

Firstly, obviously, the song is about me. Keiko was so moved by my lack of self-love, so frustrated and tormented about it, that she was driven to put pen to paper, words to verse. I picture her working late into the night, headphones on as Momo sleeps beside her, only now I see her writing about me. Finding the perfect melody, the perfect instrumental arrangement. My heart aches.

Secondly, there's something so life-affirming about seeing her up there, like this, inches away from me but light years too.

It's like she's sharing her power with the room. Sometimes you hear a great singer and you think, oh, I wish I could sing like them. But this isn't that. Instead of making me wish I was like her, Keiko makes me want to be the Keiko of whatever I do. It makes me want to rock the world of astrophysics with my own flair, my own quirks, my *own* power. It's like she's giving me permission to go after what I want, to be unapologetic and authentic, to embrace where I came from.

I don't know what this feeling is: this heat that spreads

through my chest, the raw energy pulsing in my veins, this yearning and this sense of purpose.

I stay up there at the front for the rest of the set. Haruki joins me at some point, cups his hands around my waist as I sway to *This Neverending Night* and *Rise Up*. Keiko doesn't look at me again, and I can't tell if she's mad I came. Still, I don't regret it.

When it's over, it's clear nobody wants Jaxon Zentner to take the stage. Keiko yells goodnight, and the crowd goes wild. I feel their screams in my bones.

Halfway into Jaxon's set, Haruki and I meet Keiko at the bar. When she taps me on the shoulder, I jolt like I've been electrocuted and spin around to face her. The grin on her face spreads from ear to ear. I throw my arms around her.

'I'm sorry,' she whispers, squeezing me back. 'Thank you for coming. And not hating me.'

So she wasn't mad I came.

Maybe . . . embarrassed? That I heard her song before I was supposed to? Before she made sure it was okay that she wrote about me?

I pull away. We keep our faces close so we can hear each other over the noise of Zentner's gravelly solo. She smells of the silver conditioner that comes with her hair dye. 'It's okay. Really. I'm sorry I said you were jealous.'

'It's okay.' She pauses and nibbles her lip. Her hair is kinda mussed up from our hug. 'I'm sorry for *being* jealous.'

I smirk in probably not an attractive way. 'So, you admit it.'

'Oh, shut up.' She nudges me with her hip. 'You're not a cute winner.'

I study her then, my best friend in the world, my best friend with this huge, huge talent. It fills me with pride and emotion. 'You were amazing, Kiks. Hell, amazing isn't a big enough word.'

'You're such a dork.' She drops her gaze in a bashful way, which is . . . not her usual style. 'But thanks. That means a lot.'

We just look each other then, and I don't know what she's thinking. Hell, I don't even know what I'm thinking, other than playing the lyrics to *Bones and Stardust* over and over and over in my head.

Why are you so afraid when you are the universe
And the universe is you?

I have so many questions about that song, and no real way to ask them without giving away that I know – or at least suspect – it was about me.

Haruki shuffles awkwardly beside me. Keiko doesn't even ask where Gabriela is.

I start speaking at last. 'When did you –'

'Keiko.' A heavily tattooed woman with gauged ears appears beside Kiks, a coy smile on her pixie-ish face. Her name badge says *Marieke*, and I think she's the manager of the bar. 'There's someone backstage I'd like you to meet.'

Keiko's eyes light up. 'Is it . . . ?'

Marieke shrugs playfully. 'You'll have to wait and see.'

Keiko turns back to me, twinkling. 'This could be it.'

Any disappointment I felt about having this conversation interrupted evaporates. I squeeze her hand. It's clammy and a little shaky. 'I'll text you later. I want to know *everything*.'

Not long after she heads backstage, Vati picks us up outside the venue, and the whole ride back, Haruki chatters animatedly about how amazing Keiko was, how inspired he felt. And it's weird, because I'm not jealous. The Caro of a few weeks ago would've probably been bitter that my boyfriend (STILL WEIRD) was more obsessed with my best friend's performance than with the girl sitting right next to him, but how can I be mad when that's how I feel too?

Thoughts of Keiko eclipse all else, to the point where I don't even notice when Vati picks up an Argentinian hitchhiker on the freeway.

17

When we get home after dropping Haruki off in his very fancy neighborhood, Dad whips out a breathalyzer kit and makes me blow into it, then makes me walk up and down the hallway in a straight line, all while Sirius is going to town on my hip. So just your standard Saturday evening in the Kerber-Murphy household.

I shower, take off my makeup, brush my teeth and get into bed, and by the time I do, there's a string of messages from Keiko in the group chat. (She's one of those people who sends a million short texts instead of one long one.)

SO

Guess what??

The person Marieke wanted me to meet was . . .

Wait for it

BELLA BALZER

AN ACTUAL LITERAL MANAGER

Who represents so many of my favorite artists???

Like Miranda May, Beach Street, Amelia Lovell, Joe Johnson & The Jaguars

And she honestly was so so complimentary of my set, she super GOT the gagaku stuff you know?? I could just tell she was so excited by it

ANYWAY SHE OFFERED TO REP ME!!!

I HAVE A MANAGER NOW I GUESS???

Then there's a whole bunch of celebration dance gifs. I break out into a huge grin, warmth spreading through my chest. The success feels like my own. Keiko's happiness feels like my happiness.

But then I see the reply from Gabriela:

that's cool hey! sorry i didn't make it tonight, lizzie got caught shoplifting lol what an idiot

I could kill Gabriela, actually kill her, for this response. This is the biggest thing to ever happen in Keiko's career, and all she has to say is 'that's cool hey' and a half-assed apology for bailing? Plus, why is she blowing us off to hang out with people who shoplift for the lols? Is this just what happens when old friends grow up with different interests? When they turn out to be totally different people?

The thought of that happening to me and Keiko fills me with dread. I don't think I could survive growing apart from her. I refuse to believe it's just an inevitability of getting older and going your separate ways come college.

I shake off my fear, instead focusing on how good it feels to be talking to her again, and send my own reply.

KIKS OH MY GOD!! That is seriously fuckign incredible?? So incredible I clearly cannot fuckign type! So so so happy for you, and not at all surprised. You absolutely slayed tonight! So what happens now? What does Bella do next? Ahhhhh!

I can't bring myself to respond to Gabriela, or ask any more about the shoplifting. I won't let Keiko share this moment with a basic bitch delinquent like Lizzie.

Okay so as well as managing your schedule, booking gigs, and generally making sure I'm heard by the right people, she'll also be trying to get me signed to a record label????

Which would be HUGE for me obviously

It's just such a massive show of faith you know?

It was such a risk to try out this new style and it was so so much work to get the whole set to that level, and to find musicians who could pull it off, and the fact it's been worth it is just . . . oh god I'm crying

After a little more back-and-forth with no replies from Gabriela, we take it away from the group chat and message privately.

What she writes next genuinely surprises me.

Anyway enough about me! Please update me on all your things. How's it going with Haruki? And how's the MIT application coming along? And has Vati finally managed to grow his turnips? (Not a euphemism GET YOUR MIND OUT OF THE GUTTER)

The biggest night of her life and she's asking me about how I am.

I fight the urge to clasp the phone to my heart. This is all I've wanted from her for so many years. To feel like she cares about me as much as I do about her. To feel like I am as interesting as she is.

A hollow thought strikes me around the temple. Is this just another side effect of the pill? What if it's the pheromones making Keiko write songs about me?

Or is it because the pills have influenced the way I act around Keiko? Has being more assertive with her – calling her out, running ahead without her – shocked her into seeing me?

Mind still in turmoil, I type a response.

It's going well with Haruki, I think! He's a cool guy. And my dads like him, which is good. MIT . . . ahhhhh I'm so excited and nervous about finally sending the application off, but it's coming together. Leo's looking over it right now. So weird after so many years of fantasizing about it. And no, I regret to inform you that there has been a turnip massacre. He accidentally used weed killer instead of plant food. Our backyard is a root vegetable graveyard right now.

We talk for hours, about *both* of our stuff, and I seriously wish I was with her for real. I wish I could see her face light up as she tells her mom her big news, and I wish I could run through the night with her over and over again as we fall asleep, squashed together in her bed like we always do.

I wish I could understand what's going through her head right now – and what's going through my own.

The next day, Haruki seeks special permission from my fathers. Not to marry me, for we are in high school and that would be absurd, but to take me to a cosmology event at the Wolfendale Observatory that lasts until midnight. My dads have never exactly been curfew types, but then again, I've never had the hottest guy in school ask to take me on a late-night date before, so.

As it happens, I've already done my homework so they're remarkably chill about the whole thing, even helping us prepare a little picnic basket full of black pepper cashews, boxes of freshly chopped fruit, cheese pastry twists and bottles of fizzy peach water. Just despicably cute, to be honest.

Then Vati drives us up to the observatory, tucked away in an area of National Park that's a designated Dark Sky zone. This status means the night sky is protected, and lighting controls are in place to prevent light pollution, so on a clear night, you can see what feels like the entire cosmos. We drive up the dirt track surrounded by giant elms, the sky already darkening to a dusky purple.

'Have you been here before?' Haruki asks me. We're both sitting in the back of the car, and for once, Vati is too busy swearing about potholes to eavesdrop.

'I came a lot as a kid, but not for a few years. Not since they got the new Skywatcher Equinox telescopes. You?'

Haruki shakes his head. He's staring up at the sky through the car window, an awed look already on his face. 'Nah, never. I don't know what to expect.'

'Stars.' I grin. 'A lot of them.'

We wave goodbye to Vati, who promises to chain-drink espresso so he doesn't fall asleep before picking us up at midnight. Last time he so much as touched espresso, he decided to paint the porch pillbox red, so this fills me with horror and also excitement to see what kind of state the house will be in on our return.

Trekking up to the observatory – built of smooth wood and glass to blend into the forest – I wrap my jacket tighter around me. It's a little chilly between the trees. Haruki offers me his chunky beanie hat, and I tug it gratefully over my ears.

Our footsteps crunch on the leaf-covered track, and silence settles comfortably between us. Haruki's breathing is steady and deep. The woods feel endless around us. The air is full of crisp potential. The night itself seems woven with peacefulness.

Being around Keiko lately has felt so spiky, so frenetic, so loaded. It's nice to leave all that behind for a night and just . . . be.

We show our tickets at the door of the observatory and head upstairs to the main viewing deck. Haruki lets out a long slow whistle, and deservedly so. The structure is built into the side of a hill, so not only can you see an enormous panorama of night sky, but also a plunging view of the forest-filled valley below. Telescopes jut through vast open windows, offering a 360-degree view of the National Park and the sky above it. Tonight, there's not a cloud to be seen, so even though it's not fully dark yet, the sky is already glittering with stark white stars.

'Told you,' I whisper breathlessly, stunned by the effect it still has on me. The beauty makes my bones ache.

In all honesty, this place has a lot of emotional resonance for me. It's where I first thought about the universe beyond our own tiny planet, back at the ripe old age of six. It's where I had my seventh birthday party – Keiko was the only person to turn up, and to be frank, it was probably better for it. It's where I demanded, at the age of eight, that I wanted to convert our attic into my very own observatory. Dad entertained the idea, even buying me a rudimentary telescope, but the light pollution in my town was too thick to ever really see anything.

Sharing it with Haruki feels more intimate than kissing ever has.

As it happens, we're the only weirdos who signed up to an event called Intermediate Cosmology In The Forest late on a Sunday night, so it's just us and the guide. This means we get a telescope each, and can ask as many questions as we like. I've already done this event multiple times as a kid so I don't ask anything, but Haruki has lots of thought-provoking questions, some of which neither the guide nor I can answer. I love that he does. I love the way his brain works. I love that he thinks an observatory is a cool place for a date.

It's weird, because lately, I haven't felt the Matching Hypothesis hanging over my head as much. When we first got together, I felt like a fraud, rebelling against science itself, but now it all seems so absurd to reduce a person – whether yourself or someone else – to their appearance or social status. Because when it comes down to it, Haruki and I are . . . we're extremely similar. We have the same values, the same interests, the same outlook. Same but different insecurities, same but different ambitious streak.

Not only does it now seem insulting to myself to say I don't deserve him because of the way I look, it also seems insulting to him to imply he can't look beyond that, to our values and interest and outlooks, our insecurities and ambitions. It's just . . . it's all insulting. The Matching

Hypothesis. And I hate that I ever cared about it.

After the guide has finished her talk, she asks me how my dads are doing, then leaves us to enjoy the observatory in peace. We crack open our picnic basket and feast under the stars.

There's magic in the air. For some reason, I find myself not thinking about the science behind what I'm looking at – at constellations and physics, or even how the telescopes were made. I just allow myself to enjoy the beauty, without questioning it, without interrogating it, without trying to make sense of it.

We're sitting side by side on the wooden floor, arms pressed together, when he says, 'You know, I kind of can't believe we're together.'

The me of a few weeks ago, maybe a few days ago, might've jolted at this. Might've assumed the worst, that he meant something bad by it. But I feel so at peace in so many ways, and the hurt never comes. I simply ask, 'How so?'

He crunches through a cheese twist, flakes of pastry scattering over his crossed legs. 'I just . . . well, I never felt like I wanted a girlfriend, first of all. Not until we got close.'

'What changed?' Other than boosted sex pheromones, obviously.

'I dunno.' He finishes his twist and turns to face me. 'You were just so different to the people I usually spend time with. In the best way. And I found myself wanting more and more of it.' His warm hand cups my jaw, and he peers deep into my eyes like the secrets of the known universe are hidden at the bottom. 'Being around you, talking to you. Kissing you. It's just nice, and easy, and right.'

I melt. Absolutely melt. 'I feel the same,' I murmur, closing the small gap between our lips. He sighs as I press against him, sinking into the kiss.

Eyes still closed, he rests his forehead against mine. 'I think . . . I think I love you.'

Everything in my body explodes like fireworks.

The moment. The moment I've always fantasized about but never got. It's here, and it's perfect.

'Wow,' I say, unable to fight off the grin, which in turn makes him smile too. 'I think I love you too.'

He chuckles. 'Just, like . . . not as much as I love Vati. The guy is a hero.'

Right on cue, we hear the sound of Vati's car horn, blaring through the night with no concern for the fact there's a kestrel sanctuary next door.

18

I have the dream again that night, the fourth in a row, and I wake up feeling off-kilter. Again, I don't feel fear in the face of that room anymore; just curiosity. I want to understand this integral part of myself.

It feels more significant, more meaningful, than ever, but I don't know why. I've lived with this hole in my history for so many years. Why the burning intrigue now? Why does it feel paramount?

It's raining out, and it's a nice change of scenery – not to mention good for Vati's turnip carcasses. Dad is working on his book in the study, while Vati is walking a disgruntled Sirius down by the river. They've got a sweet relationship, my dads. They don't have to do everything together all the time to prove they care about and love each other. It's just easy for them. I want that one day.

No, I say to myself, shaking away the habitual thought. *I have it already. Or at the very least, I'm well on my way.*

After reliving the night in the observatory for the millionth time, I make me and Dad cups of tea, replace all of Vati's shampoo with garlic mayonnaise, then head up to my room to buckle down.

It's a national holiday, so I'm not in school today. As I'm working on a personal essay for my college application, I find a roughly recorded version of *Bones and Stardust* on Keiko's website, and I play it in the background.

Mistake.

After seven plays in a row, I haven't written a single word of my essay. And I think I've figured out why I'm fixating on that dream.

Why are you so afraid of your own dimensions
When your dimensions are your history
There's eternity
Within you

I think what she's saying is that . . . she doesn't understand why I hate myself when I'm a combination of actual stardust and the millennia of my ancestry. Just knowing that about yourself makes you feel both miraculous and inevitable.

Yet half of that equation is a mystery to me. I understand the stardust, but not my past. I don't know who I am, on a bone-deep level. (Please refrain from any and all boning

216

jokes. This is not the time.)

Non-adopted kids raised by their biological parents just take it for granted that they can pretty easily analyze their own personality, their own body, their own personhood, in the context of their mother and father. They can say, 'I got my wit from my mom and my short temper from my dad, and the reason I have a long torso and short legs is genetics. I'm intelligent like my mom – with such an ability to retain information that I'm basically a living encyclopedia – instead of like my dad, whose logic and reasoning are sharp as a tack, but whose memory is that of a colander.'

They can do that *ad infinitum*, if they want to. And I can't. As a scientist, and as a human being, that's hard.

For nearly fifteen years, I have seen no pictures, asked no questions, and suddenly the absurdity of that strikes me. Sure, for a while I genuinely didn't care. I had two amazing dads and that's all I needed. But it's been months and months since the dreams have started to inspire this curiosity, and I just . . . let myself suffer to protect my parents' feelings. The Caro Kerber-Murphy M.O.

Same as I did with Keiko. I kept quiet about how she was making me feel, because I didn't want to ruin things between us. And yet as soon as I began asserting myself, our relationship transformed into something better than it's ever been.

Maybe that's what'll happen if I ask my dads for information about my mother. They'll respect my scientific curiosity, respect that I did the hard thing and asked them. Hell, they're maybe wondering why it's taking me so damn long. Vati could've grown enough turnips to feed the whole of Canada in the time it's taken me to pluck up the courage. You know, if he was in any way a skilled gardener, not a clown and a vegetable murderer.

It's hard putting your own needs above others', but maybe I don't even need to do that? Maybe I simply need to value my needs *equally* to others'. Instead of constantly thinking about what's best for them, I should focus on what's best for us both. Maybe that approach will finally stop me from feeling like a sidekick in my own life.

Before I can change my mind, I grab what's left of my tea and head downstairs.

'Dad, can we talk?'

He turns away from the computer and lays down his glasses. 'Sure. What is on your mind?'

Perching on the arm of the reading chair by the mahogany bookcases, I swallow hard and force the words out. 'My mom.'

I can't read his expression as he replies, 'I see.'

'I'm sorry,' I blurt out, filled with regret already.

Dad shakes his head. 'No, please, do not be. I am surprised it has taken you so long to bring this up.'

There's a taut pause as we both try to figure out how to proceed.

Dad nods gently. 'I feel your other father should be here for th—'

'You rang?' Vati waltzes in, still dripping wet from the shower, in an ancient bathrobe. 'Who put aioli in my shampoo? With the lemon juice I put in my hair for highlighting, I smell like salad dressing. Which is fine if you are a salad. But I am not. I am a man. Who smells of salad dressing.'

'Your timing is quite remarkable,' Dad says.

'I am always listening, Michael. This whole house is bugged like the headquarters of a drug ring.' He taps his ear as though there's an invisible earpiece in there. Maybe there is, you never know.

'Caro would like to talk about her mother,' Dad says softly. 'Do you think you can hold a serious conversation for more than eleven seconds?'

'Absolutely not,' Vati says. He opens Dad's desk drawer, pulls out some parcel tape, and proceeds to tape his own mouth shut. The only logical solution, I'm sure we can all agree.

'Very good,' Dad says, gesturing for his very strange husband to take a seat. He sinks into the antique leather armchair by the bookshelf.

In a small voice, I ask, 'Who was she?'

Dad leans back in his chair and sighs. Not in an angry or sad way, just like he's preparing himself to talk. 'There are parts of this story that are . . . not pleasant. I want you to be prepared for that.'

My chest starts to thud. 'I know. I think I've seen some of it in my dreams.'

Dad rubs his eyes, places his glasses on the bridge of his nose, then takes them off again. He's nervous, and it's unsettling, because he's never nervous. Vati watches him with wide eyes.

'Very well. Your mother was a woman named Annie.' His voice is steady, but not as robotic as usual. There's a warmth in it, albeit with a little tension stringing the words together.

'She was born in Tennessee and lived in Florida, where she worked as a waitress. She loved country music and horse-riding. When she fell pregnant in her mid-twenties, her long-term partner – a high-school sweetheart – left her in the lurch. She was a strong woman, and she decided to raise you without him. Unfortunately, there were complications when she gave birth. Nothing life-threatening, but a fourth-degree perineal tear, which required surgery and a long recovery time. Not easy with a newborn and no support from a partner.'

Quickly, as though to save him the trouble of saying it –

and me the trouble of hearing it — I say, 'So she put me up for adoption.'

'No.' He folds his hands together in his lap. 'This next part might be difficult to hear. If you would like me to stop at any time, please say so.'

Trembling, I mumble, 'Okay.'

'Following the surgery and the trauma it left behind, Annie became addicted to prescription painkillers. Opioids. Still, she tried to maintain a normal life, giving you the care and stability you deserved. For the first year, that was exactly what you received. But despite all her best efforts and rehabilitation programmes, Annie's drug use spiralled until she was no longer able to take care of you. I do not want to go into details, but eventually, your circumstances became so dire that social services took over your care.'

I shudder involuntarily. 'So social services just . . . put me up for adoption? What would have happened if my mom had eventually gotten sober?'

Dad's gaze drops to the ground. 'Annie died of an overdose one week after you were taken.'

My chest cracks open.

My mom's name was Annie. She was a music lover, a waitress, an addict.

She is dead now, and has been for many, many years. The grief hits me like a physical blow.

I will never, ever know her.

Vati stands up – mouth still taped shut – reaches into a hidden pocket in his wallet, and pulls out a pristine photograph of my mom bouncing me on her hip.

She is beautiful. And she looks exactly like me.

High forehead, strong jaw, narrow nose. Dark blond hair. Piercing blue eyes. A small beauty spot on her left cheek. Dimples as she smiles.

In the picture, she looks so happy that it breaks my heart. She has no idea what's to come. All she knows is the pain she's already feeling – the pain she is smiling through, because she has me in her arms.

I stare at it for so long that I stop seeing it, and then some more. Finally, Dad breaks the silence. 'Do you want to talk some more?'

A lump bobs in my throat. 'I think . . . I think I need some time. Just to think.'

He studies my face. 'Are you upset with us for keeping this from you?'

There's a vulnerability in his eyes that I've never seen before, and that's what finally caused my tear ducts to erupt.

'No! No, of course not. I-I . . . don't think it's something I could bear to know unless I was mentally prepared for it.'

Dad nods softly. 'I am glad we made the right call.'

I can't imagine what this has been like for him – for both

of them. Keeping this unimaginably painful secret from the one person it has impacted the most, and having to believe, every single day, that it's is the right thing to do.

Do they ever feel guilty? That they got to live, got to raise me, when Annie didn't? I hope not. I hope they're only ever happy to have me in my life, in the purest way it's possible to be happy, even though I understand that life is more complicated than that.

'You always make the right call,' I say, surprised by the ferocity in my voice. I need him to believe me. 'Both of you. And I will never not be grateful for it.'

Dad's face crumples, and he instantly covers it with his hands. His shoulders shake, and I know he's crying too. Despite the situation, I laugh and wrap my hands around his waist.

'Dad. It's okay,' I say, as Vati bounds over and joins in the hug. 'You're allowed to show emotion. You don't have to maintain the robot façade at all times.'

Dad sniffs into my hair. 'I have no idea what you are talking about. I am an extremely expressive person. Hollywood could write a soap opera about me.'

'I love you both so much,' I mumble through a combination of laughter and hot tears.

Dad kisses my head. 'We love you too. You have no idea how much.'

'Vrshmnrn,' says Vati through the tape.

We stay like that in a group hug for a few moments, none of us speaking or moving; just being.

And to be fair to Vati, he really does smell like ranch.

Lying in bed, I gaze at a picture I have of the three of us – Dad, Vati and me – on my phone. They are the best parents I could ever ask for. But they are not my only parents. And somehow, that makes my life richer. It makes *me* richer.

I will never, ever know my mom. Yet knowing her story has already cast my life into a new light. It has provided a new filter, a new context, that I so desperately needed.

Now, I can picture myself as an extension of her. I've never been able to do that before. My thoughts when I saw that picture were that she was beautiful, and that she also looked like me. I no longer see those things as mutually exclusive. There are a few things that have culminated in this epiphany, but I know seeing my mom for the first time is what really brought the belief home. I'm beautiful because I have her in me.

Another penny drops. Dad's obsession with my supposed alcohol addiction – it's rooted in the very primal fear that I'll meet the same fate as my mom. This new understanding fills me with love for him.

The thought crosses my mind that this is the kind of thing I should talk to my boyfriend about. He cares about me and my family and my past, and . . . he loves me. This is something he would want to know.

Something else clicks. Something so horrifying and dark that it makes me want to roar in self-loathing. Something I think I already knew, deep down in my bones, but that hasn't surfaced until now, until I finally had this context, this lens, this filter.

I'm also taking drugs, with no real knowledge of the long-term effects, no clue how addictive they are, no idea how they're impacting my life beyond the obvious. No idea how they *really* affect other people. Worse, I'm dragging someone else down with me. Someone who did *not* make this choice. I never gave him the chance.

My mind races like a helter-skelter.

Is Haruki really consenting to be with me if I'm basically using drugs to lure him in?

Okay, so I'm not drugging him, just myself. I'm boosting my natural pheromones to make him more attracted to me. Up until now, I've managed to convince myself it's no different to perfume, or make-up, or a really great haircut.

Where are the lines?

I rethink every romantic encounter I've ever had. Kevin only ever wanted to have sex with me while drunk. Sober, he wasn't interested. So . . . was he really consenting? Is it even *possible* to give consent when there's an external substance influencing your judgment?

It seems extreme to say all drunk sex is non-consensual. As Vati so often horrifyingly tells me, red wine makes him horny. Do I really think he's fundamentally incapable of giving consent after a glass or two?

Like I say, it seems like an extreme statement, but . . . god, I don't even know anymore. I guess all we can do is draw our own lines, then give other people the chance to draw theirs – and honor them accordingly, without trying to influence or shift them one way or another.

That's something I haven't afforded Haruki, and I hate myself for it.

'*I never felt like I wanted a girlfriend. Not until we got close.*'

I didn't respect his lines. He had decided that he wasn't attracted to me, and he let me down accordingly, but I was too humiliated to honor that.

Kevin didn't want to answer my texts. I didn't honor that either.

Fuck.

I was so convinced I was the victim.

Throwing my blanket off me with a new sense of resolve,

I do what I should've done a long time ago.

I take the pheromone pills to the toilet, and I flush them all away.

Then I look at myself in the mirror. Really, really look at myself. At the good, the bad, and the ugly. And I realize that for so long, I was so busy obsessing about what was on the outside that I didn't look any deeper.

Later that night, Vati comes into my room to tell me where my mom's ashes are scattered – he'd asked the adoption agency for some information on my past, in case I ever asked. Anyway, they're spread at a run-down amusement park near the coast – Annie had once told her brother it'd be funny to scatter her ashes from the top of the Ferris wheel, so the ashes would get into the candyfloss and a bunch of sticky fairground kids would end up eating her. So that's what they did.

'She sounds hilarious,' I laugh through fresh tears. 'I wish . . . '

I start to say that I wish I could've known her, but I stop myself. That's basically like saying I wish I'd been raised by her instead of my dads, and the sight of Vati's goofy face makes it an intolerable thought.

Turns out he reads my mind anyway. Perched on the edge of the bed, he squeezes my foot through the duvet, which is a bit weird, but then again he is a bit weird so it makes sense.

'*Bärchen*, it is okay. You are allowed to wish that, while also being happy that you have us. Our minds, they are complicated. That is the mustard I wish to add.'

'What?' I snort.

'My two cents, I suppose you Americans would say. You have no originality. Although Annie, she did. An amusement park. So funny. An inspiration to us all, *Bärchen*. Just like you. Anyway, this is the address of the park, if you ever want to visit her.'

After he leaves, I fondle the piece of paper. It's old, I think, the blue ink faded and the paper soft. I run my thumb over the zip code like it's a magic portal to wherever my mom is now.

I remember what I told Haruki in the diner. If I could access the sixth dimension, where you could see all possible futures, presents, and pasts in universes with the same start conditions as ours, I could theoretically move along those timelines like walking up and down a hallway, and essentially live two lives. The one I have now, with my dads and my brother and Sirius. And the one where I still have Annie. The one where she had a straightforward birth and didn't get addicted to painkillers and never overdosed.

Maybe one day we'll achieve the breakthroughs we need that will make accessing those dimensions a reality. Maybe I'll be the one pioneering those breakthroughs, and in my Nobel Prize acceptance speech, I'll tell this exact story.

And maybe none of this will happen in my lifetime. I have to learn to be okay with that too.

Suddenly, the urge to talk this through with Keiko is overwhelming. She's exactly who I need right now.

Hey. Can you come over?

It takes her a few minutes to reply.

Yo! I'm hanging with Marieke right now, but I'll be there soon as we're done

Everything okay??

The sinking disappointment is heavier than it should be. It's not just that I'm sad she can't come over, it's . . . something else.

It's the feeling of having to share her. The very same thing I yelled at her for, not so long ago.

Okay. Okay, I get it now. It's irrational and petty and it makes you feel like an actual literal toddler, but I get it. It's a primal, territorial thing. I want Keiko to just be mine.

But she's allowed to date. She's young and hot and talented and this is such an exciting time for her, so why shouldn't she be going out and having fun and sharing all this stuff with someone?

Because I want her to be doing all that with me, a small voice whispers. I shake it away, afraid to look at it head-on, afraid to ask it any more questions because truth be told, I'm scared of the answer. Especially in light of the fact that I recently learned – really, truly learned – that wanting someone doesn't mean you're entitled to them.

Oh yeah don't worry dude! I just found out some stuff about my birth mom and it's thrown me a little. Are you up for skipping school tomorrow? For a road trip out to the coast? That's where her ashes are scattered. In a theme park because she's baller.

This time, it takes forever for her to reply, and the primal, territorial feeling intensifies into a desperation I don't like one bit. I just want to be talking to her. It's a physical yearning.

But I have to stop forcing myself on people. I have to respect the lines they set themselves.

So I do the extremely mature and rational thing of trying to trick my phone into receiving a message. Leaving it lying on my bed, I go and shower, finish my essay, help Dad cook dinner, and play chess with Vati. He is truly appalling. Like imagine a chimp trying to formulate an endgame strategy that doesn't involve its opponent slipping on a banana peel. He just doesn't have the mental capacity.

Vati also keeps abandoning the game to practice his Zumba moves, complete with ad-libbed vocals from Dad, who I'm pretty sure is just repurposing *Despacito*. It's the silliest Dad has been in forever, and I wonder if lifting the burden of my mom's secret has left him feeling lighter. Anyway, I win the chess game and get a good laugh out of the festivities, so it's a successful evening all round.

I climb the stairs back up to my room, and my heart starts to pound as I anticipate checking my phone.

Sinking into my duvet, I take a deep breath and press the home button.

She replied. A lot. I beam into the fairy-lit room.

Oh wow okay

Your birth mom! That's so exciting and such a big step

How are you feeling??

And are you sure you don't want me to come over?

Also count me the hell in for a road trip although you seem to be overlooking the fact we don't have a car

If you mean 'walk' then I will disown you, don't put me down for cardio

I know you like running now which is a serious character flaw but please know I am currently arranging a lobotomy before you go full Forrest Gump

Then, when I didn't reply to any of her messages within 0.2 seconds:

Bitch if you're punishing me for being on a date right now then I swear to god I will have you arrested for the sheer HYPOCRISY and AUDACITY

Chuckling aloud to myself, I type out a response.

Okay so I'm feeling okay just kinda . . . sad, I guess. I don't know why I'm grieving for a woman I don't really remember. It just hurts and I don't understand it. But anyway. Oh yeah I didn't think the car thing through. I guess we need Gabriela, but it doesn't seem like she's super into hanging out with us at the moment. AND I'M NOT PUNISHING YOU. Get over yourself before I have you arrested for the sheer NARCISSISM and SELF-OBSESSION

The blue ticks appear immediately, then she's typing.

Dude I am so glad you just said that about Gabs

I thought it was just me being paranoid

Is it wrong that I'm upset at her for bailing on the gig?

And just like not being that enthusiastic about me signing with Bella

Like you say I do veer on the side of narcissism at all times so literally just tell me if I'm being a Mariah about it

I snort with laughter.

In 98% of cases you are in fact being a Mariah, but you're off the hook here. I was pissed at her too. She's been so distant with us lately. Maybe a road trip just the three of us tomorrow is exactly what we all need?

Her first reply is:

Roger that, amigo

Then she writes in the group chat:

Okay Gabs, we are shotgunning your presence tomorrow please

I don't care if you have to bail Lizzie out of jail or whatever

Also don't be lame and point out it's a school day

We're going on a mandatory road trip to where Caro's mom's ashes are scattered

It sounds supes morbid but her mom was actually legendary and had herself disseminated all over an amusement park so?? Hilarious

You in?

Fluffing the pillow up under my head, I can't stop smiling. Keiko just has this ability to find the levity in any situation. Nothing is too dark to laugh at. And while she does take herself and her work seriously, she's always willing to laugh at how seriously she takes it.

oh hey girl! this sounds so fun, can lizzie tag along?

A bubble of anger rises in my throat. When did we stop being enough for Gabriela? Luckily, Keiko has my back.

Like fuck she can

This is a big deal for Caro, like a really really big deal, and she needs her best friends

You are her best friend

Lizzie is not

Capiche?

After a few seconds, Gabriela replies.

lol chill that's fine i was only asking. all good. what time shall i pick you guys up?

2 0

The next morning, I lie to my dads about getting a ride to school, and Keiko meets me outside my place to wait for Gabriela to pick us up. The weekend's rain has left everything fresh and cleansed, and the rosebushes at either side of our front door glisten with the lingering dew. I am fairly sure they're fake rosebushes, actually. There is no way Vati kept real ones alive until October.

Keiko's wearing massive sunglasses, hoop earrings, and a blue-and-white striped jumpsuit that would look like shepherd pyjamas on anyone else, but on her looks effortlessly cool. She grins at me as she strolls up the driveway.

'What's up?' she says, voice full of bounce. She *loves* road trips, and her giant tote bags rustles with an impressive plethora of snacks.

'Um, *a whole lot!*'

Keiko laughs at my enthusiasm. 'I've never seen anyone so excited about a dead parent and/or a ride on some old dodgems.'

'No, not that. Did you not see the news?'

We perch ourselves on the bonnet of Vati's SUV, which is the only dry surface in sight. I can just about hear him in the living room, tapping out distress signals in Morse code.

'You'll have to be more specific, babe,' Keiko says. 'Our definitions of news differ wildly. If it didn't happen on *Real Housewives* I'm probably not up to date.'

I pull my denim jacket tighter around me. The air has a hint of fall crispness, and it's delicious. 'The twin detectors at the Laser Interferometer Gravitational-Wave Observatory just reported a burst of gravitational waves that *could* be the first detection of a black hole devouring a neutron star.'

'That sounds wild,' Keiko says, 'even to a bonafide science moron like me. What does it mean?'

'Maybe nothing.' I shrug, but there's a flicker of excitement in my belly which begs to differ. 'But it could lead to a whole bunch of new cosmic information, from precise tests of the general theory of relativity to measuring the universe's rate of expansion.'

'Man,' Keiko murmurs, looking up at the blue sky as though she might catch a glimpse right now. 'Sometimes I forget how smart you are.'

'Really? I think about how smart I am all the time.'

Keiko cackles her witchy cackle, then pulls a can of grape

soda from her tote. She taps the aluminum lid with her white acrylic nail, then opens it with a *puh-tssssh*. She hands me first swig. 'You're different lately.'

'Different how?' I ask, taking a sip of grape soda.

'Just more . . . Caro.'

I laugh and hand her the can back. 'That makes no sense.'

She takes it but doesn't drink, instead lowering her sunglasses and studying me over them like a stern fashion editor. 'I can't put my finger on it. You're walking taller or something. And when you talk about stuff . . . you're more passionate. Before when you chatted about science and whatnot, it's like you rushed through it in case you were boring us. And you're funnier. Don't get me wrong, you've always been funny. But you could tell you were holding back in case people didn't laugh.'

The words glow like fireflies, and I hold them in my head to study later, when I'm alone and can appreciate them properly.

I'd intended to tell her about the observatory, about the words Haruki and I exchanged, but for some reason, it feels like the wrong thing to share. I keep it to myself.

Gabriela pulls up, and Keiko jumps in the front seat. She won perennial shotgun in a bet with me a few years back, when I told her I didn't think she had the stomach to eat an earthworm. She did it, Vati filmed it. It might sound like we were kids, but we were literally fifteen years old. It still makes me queasy thinking about it.

We chat for a while as Gabriela follows her satnav out of town. I tell them about the run I went on this morning and how good it felt when my lungs burned in my ribcage. Keiko calls me a freak and a masochist, but in an affectionate way. Then:

'Oh,' she adds, eyes lighting up with excitement. 'I forgot to tell you, I found this cool athletics store in the city where they measure your gait and fit you with the best running shoes for your body. How cool is that? We should totally swing by on the way home and get you the right gear.'

This makes me beam like a damn lighthouse. She researched something she doesn't care about, just for me. There's no *way* she knew what gait was before looking up that store. She cares, really really cares, about the things I love. Just because I love them.

Gabriela tells us about Lizzie's stint in the mall jail as though it's the funniest thing that has ever happened to anyone, and we laugh politely, not wanting to piss on her chips, but still a little mad that she's been too busy with the crime squad to ask about Keiko's career stuff.

I agonize over whether or not to tell them about the pills. It would be so easy not to, although they'll probably find it weird when I go back to school tomorrow and everyone's totally over me. I push the thought of Haruki's inevitable 'oh my god what was I thinking' moment out of my mind.

Selfishly, I want to keep Keiko's compliments earlier for myself. I want to feel like I have full ownership of them; like I earned them fair and square.

But before I can even make the decision myself, disaster strikes. Keiko goes rooting in my purse for my spare USB cable, and pulls out a pill packet I forgot was in there.

'What's this?' she asks, frowning at the foil wrapping.

'The pill,' I lie quickly.

'Uh, why's the writing in Spanish? Are these FDA-approved? They don't look like any pill I've ever seen before.'

'It's . . . a new . . .'

'Whatever. I'm Googling it.' My heart sinks as Keiko types the words into a translator, then into Google. '"Otherwise known as pheromones, chemical (olfactory) signals are released by an organism to attract an individual of the opposite sex, encourage them to mate with them, or perform some other function closely related with sexual reproduction".' Keiko looks up from her phone. 'Wikipedia.'

I nod. 'That sums it up.'

Gabriela turns the volume down on the radio. Keiko swivels in her seat to face me, even though it causes the safety belt to cut into her neck. 'Finally, the truth.'

Now I really do stare out the window at the rolling corn

fields and peach orchards, my cheeks burning with shame. 'Yeah. So . . . the reason a ton of people in school were suddenly into me in school was because I started taking these pills that boost your sex pheromones.'

The words seem so small, considering how much I built them up, how much I convinced myself there was no way I could tell the truth. I feel weirdly lighter for releasing them.

Keiko raises her hand like we're in school. 'Where the hell did you buy these sex telephones?' she asks, still half-reading the article. 'And can I get in on that action?'

'The internet. And I flushed them down the toilet last night.'

She launches her phone into the footwell and tears into a bag of Hot Cheetos. 'What? Are you crazy?'

I chew the inside of my cheek. 'Basically, I was biologically manipulating Haruki into being into a relationship with me. I mean, was he even really consenting? Did he have bodily autonomy? It's gross.'

'You're too hard on yourself,' Keiko says. 'It's like perfume, no? Ooh, like those women who dip their finger in their own musk and —'

'Okay, yes, very good,' I say hurriedly. 'Gabs? What do you think?' I'm keen to include her in the conversation. She's not the type to force herself in there if she hasn't been directly asked something.

'I'm glad you got rid of them,' she says. 'And I disagree

242

with Keiko. I think it's pretty fucked up what you did to Haruki.'

'Fair enough. I deserve that.' It's a weird sensation, being told off by Gabriela. She normally tries to keep the peace at whatever cost. But I appreciate her honesty.

Checking her wing mirrors even though there's no traffic behind us, Gabriela adds quietly, 'Does this mean things'll go back to normal now?'

'Yes. No. I don't know,' I admit. 'I haven't seen Haruki since I ditched the drugs. Who knows whether he'll still be into me once the drugs are out of my system.'

A soft pause. Then, 'That's not what I meant.'

'Oh,' I say, frowning. 'What did you mean?'

An even longer pause. I practically hear the mental pep talk she's giving herself. Finally, she mumbles, 'I guess it's just been hard for me lately because . . . oh god this sounds so ridiculous.'

Keiko wipes her hands on her jumpsuit and turns to Gabriela, surprisingly earnest in her tone. 'I promise you, it won't. We just want to know what's going on with you.'

Gabriela stares straight ahead, hands gripping the wheel tightly. 'You both . . . you both have such big personalities these days. And I love that about you. I promise I do. But I don't have that. I'm not like that, no matter how hard I try to keep up. And I guess I just feel a little inferior sometimes. Especially lately, with Caro's . . . you know. The way you've been.'

This is not what I expected. Thankfully, Keiko recovers before I do. 'That's crazy. You don't have to be just like us in order to be our best friend. That's what makes us great. We're all different.'

'I'm sorry if I made you feel that way,' I say. 'The pills . . . they made me feel so much more confident. I guess I didn't think how that would feel for you.' Immediately I regret my apology. Keiko isn't sitting here trying to minimize herself to make Gabriela feel better. So I add, 'But this is how I want to be. From now on, even without the pills. More like myself. I hope you can be okay with that.'

'Of course,' Gabriela says, but it sounds forced. 'Just . . . don't go thinking I'm boring, okay?'

'You're not boring,' I insist. 'I know there's a delightful little weirdo beneath that perfect makeup.' Then, realizing Kiks is typing furiously on her phone, I add, 'Keiko, what are you doing?'

'Writing to the manufacturers of your miracle pills. I think I've nailed it.'

I take the phone and read it aloud. '"Your scientists were so preoccupied with whether or not they could, they didn't stop to think if they should." Plus a whole bunch of dinosaur emojis.'

Keiko and I laugh until we cry, and Gabriela watches us through the rearview mirror with a wistful combination of affection and resignation. And in that moment, I can tell she's not done with what she wants to say to us.

Wiping away a rogue laughter-induced tear, I say softly, openly, 'Is there anything else, Gabs?'

Now she really does look uncomfortable, but she perseveres, and I appreciate the effort that takes. 'While we're being honest, I still want to hang out with the cheer squad. More than I do now. I know they're not your kind of people, but I really like them. And they like me, I think. And I feel good when I'm around them.'

Subtext: she doesn't feel good when she's around us.

And I understand. I think of her face when Ryan couldn't stop staring at me, the tears in her eyes when Keiko steamrolled her for the millionth time. The guilt is heavy on my chest.

We did this. We pushed her away. But when the only way to bring her back is to round off our edges, to turn down our volume . . . is that really friendship at all?

I don't know anymore. A few months ago, I'd have undoubtedly apologized and made extra sure that I wasn't being Too Much. I'd have expected Keiko to do the same and got mad when she didn't.

Now . . . it doesn't seem that simple. There must be a way to make sure you're being yourself while also not hurting others, not being obnoxious, not crossing lines. Not steamrolling or stealing attention that isn't rightfully yours. But it's a hard balance to strike, and since I'm pretty new to the idea of being myself, I don't have all the answers yet.

Besides. Consent is all about boundaries, and respecting each other's lines. Honoring the decisions other people make without trying to influence them one way or the other. I guess that goes for friendships, too. We have to respect what Gabriela wants.

All I can say in the moment is this:

'Love you, Gabs.' I lean forward in my seat and rest my hand on her small shoulder. 'No matter what.'

Her reply comes out a little choked, as her shoulder sinks with relief. 'Love you too.'

So I guess this is it. The thing I've been fearing the most – the landscape of our friendships shifting as we prepare to go our separate ways. I spent so long agonizing over losing Keiko that I missed what was right in front of me. Gabriela doesn't feel at home in our trio like she once did.

It's painful, of course it is, but I'm actually more okay with it than I expected to be. When it comes down to it, I'd rather Gabriela was happy hanging out with people she feels comfortable around than know she's hanging out with us and feeling shitty.

Growing up and becoming who you really are comes with

more challenges than I ever expected. The more unapologetically yourself you become, the more chance you have that people won't like it. Even your best friends. And only you can know whether that's the dice you're willing to roll.

21

We reach the amusement park and I burst out laughing. It's the most ramshackle hodgepodge of rides and kiosks I've ever seen – peeling paint and faded signs and blinking lights as far as the eye can see.

Despite the absurd quantity of junk food we ate in the car, Keiko and I both buy candyfloss, and Gabriela eyes it jealously until she finally caves and buys herself a small cone too. We walk around chatting and pointing out funny things we see – seagulls eating fries, three raccoons squabbling over a squashed ice-cream cone, two middle-aged folk getting to second base behind the Haunted Mansion.

We take a ride on the bumper cars and the log flume, then I veto the Scrambler because extreme motion sickness is not my idea of a good time. That may sound unreasonable and absurd, but it's true. In any case, Keiko and Gabriela have a great time being flung around in the air at a billion miles an hour, so each to their own.

When the sun gets high in the sky, we find a patch of grass near the Ferris wheel and lay out a picnic blanket Gabriela had in the trunk of the car. We all lie looking up at the Ferris wheel, pale autumn sun shining down on our log-flume-soaked clothes.

'Do you want to talk about your mom?' Keiko asks. Her right arm is pressed against my left. Gabriela lies on my other side, a few inches away.

'No,' I say quietly. 'I think I want her to be just mine for a while.'

Gabriela asks, 'Does it feel like she's here? In the air?'

I think about it; try to feel some kind of vibration that lets me know she's around, watching over us. But there's nothing. All I feel is the breeze in the air, the scratch of the blanket beneath me, and Keiko's skin on mine. 'I don't think so,' I admit. 'Maybe I'm too much of a science cynic to believe in that stuff. Souls existing after we're gone, and all that. But it's nice to be somewhere that had significance to her. Makes me feel like I know her, if only a little.'

Then, something funny happens.

Keiko moves her hand just slightly, so her knuckles graze mine. Then, slowly and cautiously, she links her pinky finger through mine.

Something flutters in my belly. We've held hands before, and hugged, and linked arms, and all that intimate best-friend stuff. But the flutter . . . the flutter is new.

The moment is broken too soon, and it leaves me yearning.

What is happening?

'Hey, do you wanna ride on the carousel?' she asks.

Gabriela stifles a yawn. 'I think I'm gonna nap here for a bit.'

'Caro?' Keiko says, and there's a weight to my name that makes me think she really wants me to come with her.

'Sure,' I say softly, rocking forward on to my haunches, then standing up with a creak of the knees. I offer Keiko a hand up, and she takes it. When our palms touch, the flutter takes off once more.

There are barely any kids around, on account of the fact that this is a derelict hellscape-comma-raccoon-sanctuary, so Keiko and I take the fanciest white horses we can find on the carousel with worrying about being those weird old ladies who batter children for the best seats in the park.

The ride starts up with a heaving groan that sounds like a thousand horses dying at once, and soon we've picked up speed. By speed I mean we're going at around a quarter of a mile per hour. But still.

'Hey, so, here's a question,' Keiko says, bobbing up and down as the ceramic horse simulates a gallop.

'Shoot,' I say, and the look on her face makes me nervous.

'The pills you were taking.' She fiddles with her

French-plaited lilac braids. 'The sex telephones. Did they . . . do they . . . are they effective on girls too?'

I suddenly feel dizzy despite the lackadaisical speed of the carousel. Is she asking what I think she's asking?

My pulse roars in my ears. Okay, stay calm. Don't get ahead of yourself. It's just a question. Besides, she's dating Marieke. She's probably just checking I won't steal Marieke's attention the way I did Ryan's.

'I'm not sure,' I say carefully. 'I've had trouble figuring out the rules. In the beetles, the pheromones only worked on the male of the species. But it seems a lot more complicated in humans.'

I can't tell if this was what she wanted to hear or not, and I only just manage to avert my gaze before she catches me staring at her impenetrable face.

'Oh.' She runs a white acrylic nail down the horse's pink mane. 'I was kind of hoping you'd say like . . . definitely yes.'

The thudding in my chest is so loud I'm amazed she can't hear it. 'Why?'

'I . . . I don't know, Caro.' I've never heard her so unsure, so cautious. 'The things I said earlier, about you being more . . . everything. All of it has me a little confused. Feeling confusing things. For, um . . . for you.'

The flutter is there again, threatening to lift me off my perch. 'Keiko —'

'I feel like I'm losing my mind,' she says, voice cracking with emotion. 'You're Caro. *Caro*. My best friend since forever. Am I . . . am I crazy? Are you . . . do you . . . god, what am I asking?'

Shaking so hard I have to grip the horse's neck as though attempting to strangle it with my bare hands, I say, 'What *are* you asking?'

'This thing.' She presses a hand to her chest. 'This new thing between us. Is it really there? Or am I going crazy?'

The whirling scenery around us intensifies. It feels like my entire world hangs on this answer. I need to get it right. I need it to *be* right.

And the truth is, I no longer understand my feelings for Keiko.

So many of the things I used to find frustrating about her – the narcissism, the relentless banter, the self-assurance – I now find comforting. Inspiring, even. She's so unapologetic. Maybe now that I'm starting to feel that way too, I'm no longer threatened by it. It no longer reminds me of what I'm not, but instead shows me what I could be if only I let go of my insecurities.

It's intoxicating. *She's* intoxicating. Being with her . . . it ignites something in me. But I don't know whether I idolize her or covet her. Whether I want to be her, or be like her, or be with her – or whether it's all of those things at once.

I love her. I know that. I'm just not sure what shape the love takes; whether it's platonic or familial or something new and terrifying.

I fluttered when she touched me.

When I heard the song, something long dormant awoke.

The small kindnesses I always wanted from a relationship . . . I get them from her. She calls me beautiful and sends me science stuff, she makes me terrible brownies and researches where to buy the best running shoes. She writes songs about me and skips school to go on road trips to visit my dead mom. She's been doing that stuff since kindergarten, and I've been taking it for granted when I should've realized it was *everything*.

This is impossible to wrap my head around.

I used to think love was a precise blend of biology and chemistry. Lust is governed by both estrogen and testosterone. Attraction is driven by noradrenaline, dopamine and serotonin. Long-term attachment is governed by a different set of hormones and brain chemicals: oxytocin and vasopressin. Each of these chemicals works in a specific part of the brain to influence lust, attraction and attachment.

It's all very neat, right? It's comforting in its simplicity. It exists purely in dimensions we can comprehend.

But maybe . . . maybe love is physics.

No matter how astrophysicists crunch the numbers, the

universe doesn't add up. Even though gravity is pulling inward on space-time, the universe keeps expanding outward faster and faster. It doesn't make sense. So astrophysicists have proposed an invisible agent that counteracts gravity: dark energy.

Dark energy is a cosmological constant. An inherent property of space itself. It has negative pressure driving space apart, so as space expands, more space is created, and with it, more dark energy. Based on the observed rate of expansion, scientists know that the sum of all the dark energy must make up almost seventy percent of the total contents of the universe. Seventy percent. There's more dark energy than there is anything else, right? But no one knows how to look for it. Nobody knows what it *is*.

Like the universe, my feelings for Keiko have expanded in a way I cannot decipher or pinpoint or analyze with simple science or logic. Through some kind of dark energy, those feelings have expanded beyond all recognition. And there's no way to wrap my fingers around that dark energy to see how it feels, no way to find the words to describe it, no way to put it under a microscope and examine its parts.

The way I feel about Keiko is dark energy in action. Maybe all love is.

And yet.

And yet, and yet, and yet.

The pills. What if this *is* a side effect?

What if I tell Keiko how I feel, and what if we decide to explore this new and terrifying dark energy . . . and then in a few days, the pills leave my system, and Keiko realizes she was under their influence all along? Could my heart really take that? Or would it shatter into a million pieces, like an asteroid slamming into earth?

Worse still, what if *I* realized that *I* was only feeling that way because of the pills? I could never break her heart like that. Never.

I have to be sure about this.

The silence has stretched for an eternity. The carousel slows down, but I toss some more coins at the operator to keep it running. Keiko's eyes flicker from me to the horse to the blur of ramshackle amusements around us.

I've never seen her look so vulnerable. It reminds me of Dad, right before he broke down in tears. There's something so gut-wrenching about seeing someone so strong, so stoic, reveal the chinks in their armor. It's even more gut-wrenching *being* that chink, but not in an entirely bad way.

'Keiko,' I start, voice wobbly. 'I don't know what to say. Because the truth is, I don't know. I –'

'Okay,' she says hurriedly. 'Don't worry about it.'

'No! Keiko. I didn't mean –'

'Seriously, it's okay.' She waves her hands, a frantic

gesture for me to stop talking. 'It was a crazy thing to say. Please can we just . . . not?'

'But I want to talk about it.' I hate how pleading I sound. It reminds me of the desperation I used to feel all the time. Panic rises in my gullet. Fear of fucking up this thing I never even knew I wanted.

'I can't, Caro.' Keiko shakes her head and starts disembarking from her horse, even though the carousel is still rolling. 'It's too humiliating. I should never . . .'

Before I can say another word, she's leaped off the spinning carousel, landed cat-like on the grass, and disappeared in the direction of the public bathrooms, hand over her mouth like she's trying to stop something from spilling out.

'Wait!' I call after her, scrambling to get off my horse too, but in all the panic and heightened emotion, I stumble and slam to the base of the carousel with an enormous thud. Before I know it, my head is lolling dangerously off the edge, staring up at the sky, and my feet are tangled in the hooves.

I'm trapped, relying only on my core strength to keep me on the carousel instead of plunging neck-first to the ground, which is far from an ideal way in which to plunge.

As I scream, which to be honest sounds more like a yodel, I hear Gabriela call my name, burst out laughing when she sees me, then yank out her phone, probably to record the situation for posterity.

By the time the operator realizes the life-threatening-stroke-hilarious situation and manages to bring the ride to an emergency stop, Gabriela is apoplectic with hysteria. Even I'm laughing as I'm hauled from my predicament, my abs burning as much as my cheeks.

And my first and only thought, above the pain and shame, is this:

God, I wish Keiko had been here to witness that.

In the awkwardly quiet car ride home, the lyrics to *Bones and Stardust* play on a loop in my head.

> *You are bones and you are stardust*
> *And you must, you must not betray*
> *Your reflection, your dimensions*
> *Not to mention*
> *The love that burns inside you*
> *Like bones and stardust*

I owe so much to that song. Without it, I might never have had the final nudge I needed to ask Dad about my birth mom. And knowing what I do about her, about where I came from . . . it makes me feel more whole. The gap of knowledge there used to be in me has now been filled – with grief, yes, but at least grief is not the absence of anything. It's the presence of almost every emotion there is.

I owe that to this song, and what this song represents.

'Hey,' I say slowly, daring myself to say the words. 'I have an idea.'

Keiko looks at me through the wing mirror. Her eyeliner is a little smudged. 'Always dangerous. Go.'

I take a deep breath. 'I want to get a tattoo.'

Keiko abandons all melancholy and swings around wildly in her seat. Gabriela almost crashes the car into a tree. 'When? Now?'

'Well, not right this very instant,' I say. 'Unless you've got a ballpoint pen and a razor.'

Keiko reaches into her tote and pulls them out. 'I have both of those things.'

'Shit. You called my bluff.'

Keiko studies me, tracing her gaze across my face, searching my eyes for signs that I'm joking. 'Forreal though, are you serious? Want me to ask Marieke where she gets hers done?'

Managing to avoid flinching at Marieke's name, I grin and say, 'Do it.'

Turns out Marieke knows a place that doesn't check ID. Which is how I find myself in a tiny little tattoo parlor covered in sailor-style wallpaper, where a very large white man is having one of his very large white arms inked entirely black while crying a lot. I don't know why you wouldn't just buy a black morphsuit if that's the aesthetic you're going for.

Gabriela drops us off and goes to hang out with Lizzie, and I'm kind of glad she's not here to get all judgy about the clientele.

A manic pixie dream girl with a necklace tattooed around her throat sits me down for a health consultation. True to Marieke's word, she doesn't ask how old I am. I tell her what I want, and she goes through the back to start sketching. I sip on a soda to calm my nerves, while trying not to look at Keiko and Marieke sitting super close to each other on the cracked plum leather sofa opposite me. They're watching something on Marieke's phone, arms pressed together like mine and Keiko's were just a few hours ago.

My stomach roils with jealousy. I've never felt like this about Keiko's love life before, and maybe that's because she's never properly dated anyone, or maybe my feelings are only shifting now, or maybe it's that my jealousy was misplaced all along – I thought I was jealous of Keiko being able to get whoever she wanted, when really I was jealous of the girls she was with. I just didn't know how to admit it to myself.

God. I feel like the world's biggest hypocrite after I lashed out at Keiko for feeling the same about me and Haruki.

I think back to our argument on the sidewalk outside school, when I called her out on her jealousy over all the attention I was getting. She insisted that wasn't it. '*Nice to know how little you think of me. No benefit of the doubt here, right?*'

I was so sure she was angry because I was right. I didn't stop to wonder whether she was telling the truth; whether there *was* another reason for her jealousy. She wasn't jealous of me. She was jealous of Haruki, and the relationship he was developing with me.

And the song . . .

It fits. That's when she was starting to realize how she felt.

And most surprisingly of all?

It makes me smile. And it makes me *excited*. It makes me realize how badly I want these feelings, this thing between me and Keiko, to be real.

Right here, right this second, I want to drain all the blood from my body just so the pheromones are gone, and I can know for sure. However, that is a slightly dramatic thing to do, so I must gather some self-control and wait this out.

Watching Keiko with Marieke now, panic crests in my lungs. What if it's too late by the time I finally know for sure?

Before I can torture myself by rolling around in these thoughts, the tattoo artist comes back through and shows me her design.

It's perfect. I nod.

Yes.

This is the first time I have ever broken a rule in my life. I feel giddy, and suddenly understand the rush people chase when they do shit like shoplifting. The adrenaline is intoxicating.

'You want us to come with you?' Kciko asks, looking up from the sofa.

'No. No, it's okay,' I say. 'I'm doing this for me.'

The words make Keiko smile in a way that makes me melt. Like she's proud of me. Like she respects me. Like she's . . . in awe of me.

Knowing someone is awestruck by you? It's everything. It's the feeling I've been seeking all along, I realize. Except I sought it from the wrong person.

The tattoo artist leads me through some back doors into a bigger space that smells of disinfectant and, worryingly, rum. There's eighties rock playing on a vintage radio, and the buzz of the gun as it colors in yet another inch of the very large white man's arm. He winces hard as the needle traces over his elbow. I shudder. Can I really do this?

I think of running until my lungs are on fire, and the kind of sweet pain that feels entirely different to cramps or a migraine. I guess the fact it's pain you're choosing makes a difference, and that's exactly what this is going to be. I can do it. I want to do it.

After she's finished shaving the inside of my forearm, the tattoo artist disinfects the area with clear gel, then applies the design from the transfer paper on to my skin. It looks amazing.

I can't wait for it to be real.

Nerves clamp around my stomach like a fist, and I chew a fizzy worm from the bag Keiko gave me. Apparently you have to keep your blood sugar up while getting a tattoo so you don't pass out. It probably defeats the point to eat the entire bag before the session even starts, but hey, I've always been the type of chick who finishes her popcorn before the trailers are finished rolling, and today is no exception.

'Ready?' the tattoo artist asks.

'Ready,' I say, wishing I could keep the shake out of my voice.

The gun starts to buzz, and she presses it into my skin. Although the sensation gives me a shock – maybe because I'm too hyped up with anticipation – it's actually not that bad. Just like a sharp scratch.

After she finishes the outline, I've settled into the feeling and managed to steady my breathing, so I relax as best I can. I ask the artist about how she got into tattooing, what her favorite styles are, and which tattoos she'd ban forever. She shoots an eye roll at the very large white man at this last question, and I know she hates blackout.

It takes both more and less time than I expect. More because it hurts, and it's hard to be in consistent pain over a prolonged period of time, but also less, because how can a piece of art that's going to be on your body forever only take an hour?

When it's done, though, it's all worth it. I can't stop staring. It's everything I wanted it to be.

Inked in black, the top half is an elm tree, and the bottom half is a cluster of DNA helices woven together like tree roots. Then in white, there's a smattering of tiny stars around the tree's canopy – so light against my pale skin that you have to really, really look in order to see it.

It's not the most subtle design in the world – the DNA obviously represents my mom, my origins, my genes, while the elm represents the life I've grown in South Carolina with my dads, both with stardust all around – but I'm done being subtle. I'm done hiding who I am.

I fucking love it.

When I stand up from the chair, I feel a little woozy, but the lightheadedness fades into sharp focus when I return to the lobby and Keiko leaps to her feet to greet me.

'Oh my god.' Keiko gasps as she gets close enough to study the intricate lines, the glittery white stardust. 'Dude! It's amazing.'

Marieke nods approvingly. 'Yeah, man, it's awesome. That's your first ink?'

'Yeah.'

'Respect!'

'Thanks,' I say, as the tattoo artist begins wrapping the

area in cling film to keep it clean. 'Keiko's song gave me the inspiration.' I try to meet Keiko's eye, but she's just staring at the ink on my arm. I can't read her expression at all.

'God, right?' Marieke gushes. 'Girl is super talented, like you have no idea. She's goin' places.'

This irks me. I may not be in the music biz, but that doesn't mean I don't understand how great Keiko is. How dare Marieke assume she knows more about my best friend's music than I do?

Clearly this journey of self-discovery has not made me any less petty.

22

My dads' responses to the tattoo are greedy, in that they each have roughly three different reactions in the space of twenty seconds.

Dad oscillates wildly from 'You are underage, this was highly irresponsible' to 'Has it been adequately disinfected? Nobody likes a mouldy appendage' to 'It is . . . very beautiful. Ahem. Excuse me.' The last one is him realizing what all the different elements of the design mean, and struggling to disguise how touched he is.

Vati shrieks like a banshee during childbirth, inexplicably retrieves the fire extinguisher from the kitchen, then yells, 'You are a wild child! Caro Kerber-Murphy does not leave the church in the village! Michael, can you believe this? Our daughter has a bird! And she most certainly does not have all her cups in the cupboard.'

Dad shoots me a look like Tim staring at the camera on *The Office*, and I return the deadpan glare. 'I swear he's just doing this to mess with us now,' I mutter, but with affection. Vati makes a strange giddy-up sound.

'Did you go to the tattoo parlor alone?' Dad asks. 'I hope you did not witness any drug transactions.'

'Not all tattooists are drug dealers,' I say patiently. 'And I went with Keiko, and her . . . friend. Marieke.'

'Where was Gabriela? Did you not drive with her this morning?'

'I . . . I don't think she wants to be best friends with us any more.' The words feel heavy on my tongue. 'Like, we're still cool. Nothing huge happened or anything. It's . . . we're just growing apart, I guess.'

'Well, that is hard.' Dad nods sagely. 'But it is also life.'

'Indeed,' Vati agrees. 'Who knows why the geese go barefoot?'

Dad outright ignores this. 'Caro, I am proud of you for keeping a level head. If one can indeed consider permanently scarring oneself "level-headed". Which I am not sure one can.'

Vati gesticulates wildly. 'Michael, I tell you this all of the time. Our daughter, she is wise. She knows that everything has an end. Only the sausage has two.'

And then my soul leaves my body as Dad says, 'Felix, must I retrieve the ball gag from the bedside cabinet?'

'OH BABY!' yells Vati, and he's so excited that he grips

the fire extinguisher too hard. It erupts directly into Dad's face, snapping his glasses clean in half and giving him a delightful handlebar moustache.

Why are parents.

Gabriela messages me a few hours later.

hey. so, the pills. is that why Ryan couldn't keep his eyes off you? at the diner

My insides squirm. I wonder if she put two and two together immediately, or whether she's just figured it out now. In any case, as uncomfortable as it may be, I'm glad of the chance to come clean. To let her know it wasn't her fault, or Ryan's fault. It was mine and mine alone. Facing the music is going to hurt, but honestly, I think I deserve a little hurt at this point.

God, I'm sorry Gabs. Yes. I fucked up.

I want to add so many things to the end of that text, about how awful I felt and how I'd take it all back if I could. But I don't want to paint myself as any kind of victim, to focus on my discomfort instead of hers. I've been a shitty friend enough lately.

oh okay that makes sense lol. it's just like . . . why did you keep taking them after that? after you knew what could happen? was your thing with Haruki worth risking me and Ryan's happiness?

Dropping my head into my hands, I shudder. God, I knew it was bad at the time. I knew I was being selfish and gross and I knew Gabriela deserved better. But having it laid out so plainly by a girl who'd rather die than hurt her friends . . . it's agonizing.

Past me was selfish and gross and you deserved better. I'm so, so sorry, Gabs. I should've stopped the second I realized what was at stake. I promise, I'm going to do better. I'm going to stop using self-loathing and self-pity to justify my shitty actions. Even if our relationship is going to be a little different going forward, I really need and value you in my life. Still, I understand if you can't see past this. It's so much to forgive.

I hover over the keyboard for an eternity before hitting send. It doesn't seem complete, my text, but I truly don't know what else to say.

it's okay lol you're so hard on yourself. nobody's perfect,

hey? I think I just need a bit of time to figure some things out, is that alright?

That's more than alright. Take all the time you need.

A few minutes later, her reply dings.

thanks. but Caro, please . . . you need to tell Haruki the truth. if you don't, I will. okay?

The thought sends a spike of anxiety lancing through my gut, but I know she's right. I owe him that much.

Since I can't do anything about Keiko or Haruki or any of my myriad other problems until I see them in person tomorrow – without the influence of the pills – I decide to have a self-care night, since I am apparently that kind of person now. I understand that for most people this would involve bath bombs and fancy candles, but for me it's hot cocoa and science documentaries while on Skype with my brother.

Leo cares about very little else but science, which is pretty annoying when you're trying to engage with him in a normal human manner, but is ideal for right now, when all I want to do is escape from my normal(ish) human issues. I could tell him about my journey to the place where my mom's ashes are scattered – he's adopted too, though not from Annie – but honestly I'm just exhausted. Plus he's never shown any interest in finding his biological parents, and I doubt he'd understand my desire to do just that.

Instead we chat about MIT while we watch a program on the Great Filter.

If you haven't heard of it, the Great Filter is a theory about why the universe seems so filled with potential for life, yet we haven't really found any outside our own. It posits that somewhere between pre-life and an advanced civilization capable of colonizing the stars, there's a Great Filter that stops them and ends life.

This could mean one of three things. Either we've already passed the Great Filter, unlike other civilizations on other planets. Or we're the first, meaning conditions in the universe are only now life-friendly, and we're among many on our way to the capability of colonization. Or we haven't hit the Filter yet, meaning we are, for lack of a better word, fucked. If this one is true, it means finding life or proof of life on Mars or Europa would be awful news because it would almost certainly mean the Filter is still ahead of us instead of behind us.

Caro Kerber-Murphy: here with your daily dose of existential doom.

A bit like my obsession with black holes, Leo loves theories about other life forms in the universe, and the reason we haven't made contact with aliens yet. His favorite is the Fermi Paradox, which goes like this: say there's an anthill in the middle of the forest. And right next to the anthill, humans are building a ten-lane super-highway. Would the ants be able to understand what a ten-lane super-highway is? Would the ants be able to understand the technology and the intentions of the beings building the highway next to them? Probably not.

So, when humans are searching for alien life, we're the ants. It's not that we can't pick up the signals from Planet X — it's that we can't even comprehend what the beings from Planet X are, or what they're trying to do. Our brains and our technologies just aren't advanced enough.

Honestly, my brother has a lot of flaws, but a low IQ is not one of them. I'm always surprised he chose ChemEng over physics, because he's like me — obsessed with big ideas and how we can prove them.

Big ideas like love, and what it really is.

I remember what I hypothesized earlier, about love being a form of dark energy; an indecipherable catalyst for growth. I posit my theory to Leo, keeping Keiko's name out of it, maintaining perfect academic objectivity. Kind of.

Leo is silent as he mulls this over, the light of his TV flickering over his face. His emotional intelligence is not great, so I'm genuinely curious as to what his reaction will be. Eventually, he rubs the bridge of his nose and says, 'I believe it was Professor Lawrence Krauss who once stated that we kill the universe every time we look at dark energy. According to his theory, we keep the universe unstable and decrease its lifespan as we continuously observe it.'

His meaning goes unsaid: we do the same to love. The more we study it, poke holes in it, try to reduce it to a formula . . . the more damage we do.

Whoa.

'Thanks,' I say quietly. 'That helps.'

'Are you in love, Caro?' he asks, and it surprises me, because he's not theorizing about my molecular makeup but instead about an actual human experience.

'I don't know,' I admit. 'Maybe I've been overthinking it.'

The next day, my heart hammers in my throat as I walk down the hallway to my locker.

Nobody looks.

Mateo, Nafisa and Zane are arguing about a chess tournament outside study hall, and none of them see me as I pass.

Samira and Khalil continue to make out without interruption.

Ryan delivers the egg and cheese bagel to Gabriela's locker. He doesn't look up as I walk past, but she does, and smiles kindly before turning back to him. I remember what I thought back in the diner, about how you can still appreciate someone's beauty even if you have a romantic partner. It's when you act on it that it's a problem. And even though Ryan was kind of a jerk that night, in more ways than just ogling me, I'm glad their relationship survived it. Gabriela deserves to be happy, and most of the time, that's exactly what Ryan makes her.

Mr Chikomborero nods to me, but in a way that suggests he's impressed by my running and/or the ability to channel the Holy Spirit – not because he's aroused in any way.

The pills are out of my system. Everyone ignores me the way they used to.

And it feels strangely like . . . a relief. Like I'm free to just exist.

A deep sense of rightness comes over me. This is how it was always meant to be. Some of the tension, the pressure, that has been building in me over the last however many weeks starts to dissolve.

And yet despite it all, I'm desperately afraid. I'm afraid that this self-worth I've found will fade over time without the pheromone boost. I'm afraid that being rejected by Haruki will reopen old wounds, and send me back to square one. And most of all, I'm afraid that Keiko's feelings for me will disappear too.

I'm so fucking scared.

My hand shakes as I swivel my locker combination, screwing it up at least four times before it finally opens and sends textbooks careening out of the locker and all over my feet. I bend down to pick them up, and as I'm doing so, a pair of gray trainers I immediately recognize appear beside me. Before I know it, Haruki is next to me on the dirty-ass hallway linoleum, handing me a cinnamon roll and scooping the textbooks up into his arms.

As I take the warm cinnamon roll, I remember all those weeks ago promising myself I'd never take it for granted. But I have been. I do. It's crazy what becomes normal, and how fast it does.

This might be the last cinnamon roll he ever brings me. After our night in the observatory, the thought breaks me in two.

'You know, since we're in love and all, we really need to exchange numbers.' He stands up and grins, and I catch a whiff of his clean laundry smell, cut through with expensive aftershave. 'I've been going crazy not being able to talk to you since Wolfendale.'

'There's always Instagram,' I point out, trying to keep my tone neutral, braced for what's about to happen.

He winces as he puts my textbooks back in my locker. 'Yeah, but our last conversation on there was so awk—'

As he turns to face me, he stops and frowns. He tilts his

head to the side and looks me up and down, and I swear I can almost feel the head-scratch brewing.

The temptation to stare at the ground is overwhelming. The temptation to slip back into my old ways, to be apologetic, to hide. But as painful as it is, I won't let myself. I've come too far to dissolve in front of my own boyfriend – if that's even what he is anymore. So instead I force my chin up, stop slumping my shoulders, meet his eyes. Smile like everything is fine. Like I'm the me he's spent the last several weeks starting to really like.

And preparing myself to be fine either way. Because as long as I'm respecting his boundaries, I know I'm being a good person. A better person than I have been for some time now.

'Everything okay?' I ask breezily. (I know. Things always go so well when you attempt breeziness.)

Haruki narrows his eyes. 'Yeah, it's just . . . you seem different.'

Don't flinch, don't flinch, don't flinch. Think of bones and stardust. 'Different how?'

'I don't know,' he says slowly.

'Okay!' I chirp, and busy myself rearranging my locker, giving him space to work through what's happening.

'Did you cut your hair?' he asks, still in some kind of weird confused trance.

'Nope,' I say. 'Same split ends as ever.'

'Did you do a makeup?'

'. . . Do a makeup.' Seriously. Why are boys.

'Yeah. You know, like Gabriela and her thing.'

I shake my head. 'Also nope.'

I close the locker slightly too sharply, and Haruki flinches a little. It seems to snap him from his reverie, and his strict posture relaxes somewhat, like he's melting into the moment. He smiles and says, 'Whatever it is, I like it.'

Wait. What?

I blink. 'You do?'

'Yeah. I feel like . . . I dunno.' His cute dimples materialize. 'Like I'm properly seeing you or something. I know that sounds . . . yeah.'

The nervous cramping in my chest dissolves into something soft and fluttery. 'No, it's sweet. Really sweet.'

How is this happening?

Has Haruki Ito actually developed real feelings for me?

If so . . . how? Why?

And in that moment I know – I really, really know – that it's because I have a sense of self-worth I've never had before.

There's no reason he *shouldn't* develop real feelings for me.

Not all that long ago, I was so hung up on the Matching Hypothesis. The idea that two people are more likely to form a successful relationship if they're equally desirable. Yet maybe a more accurate thesis is that two people are more likely to form a successful relationship with someone who *believes* themselves to be equally desirable.

Stop hypothesizing! I yell at myself internally. *Remember what Leo said!*

Just be here, with Haruki, right now, and let yourself feel how you feel.

And I feel . . . wrong. Because even though I'm deliriously relieved and happy that he loves me without the pills, I know I still need to tell him the whole truth. If I don't, Gabriela will.

So I tell him. All of it. The rest of the world disappears as I do.

He listens, and watches, and thinks. I can't gauge his reaction at all. I can't tell if he's furious or hurt or confused, or a combination of all three. I can't tell if he sees it just like perfume, like Keiko did, or whether his mind goes straight to the moral implications, like Gabriela.

When I finally finish, the bustling corridor reappears around us, and yet I still can't read his expression.

'Thank you for telling me the truth.'

'I owed you that much. I'm so sorry, Haruki.'

'And they're out of your system now? The pills?'

'Yeah. Totally. Talk to me. Are you angry?'

'I don't know. Yeah. A little.'

'You have every right to be.'

'Did you just view me as a science experiment?'

'What? No! God, no. Of course not. I've always . . . this makes me sound creepy, but, yeah. I fell in love with you long before you fell for me. It was always real, for me. And you were never, never an experiment.'

'God, I'm so confused.'

'Yeah?'

'Yeah. Because, like, on one hand it feels like you tricked me. I didn't want a relationship.'

'I know. And it's fucked up that —'

'I didn't want a relationship, but now the thought of not being with you is . . . god, I can't bear it. I meant every word of what I said at Wolfendale.'

'I did too.'

'This sucks.'

'I know.'

'But I still want you. Want to be with you.'

'Yeah?'

'Do you mind if I kiss you?' Haruki asks softly, stepping in until I can smell the vanilla latte on his breath.

'Yes. I mean. No. I —'

The kiss is tender and sweet, with heat underneath that I can't identify as anger or passion or both.

There's a clatter at my feet, and I look down in surprise. It's a Tupperware box, filled with half-baked brownies. Walking away in the other direction are lilac hair and soft curves.

She saw.

There's a clawing sensation in my chest, a ravaging panic that feels feral.

What if I've lost her what if I've lost her what if—

And that's when I realize. I never felt this level of carnal fear at the thought of losing Haruki. It was a sad resignation, but it didn't feel like this. It didn't feel like my own heart was about to destroy me unless I fixed it. It didn't *hurt*.

Deep in my soul, I know I have to make the painful decision.

I know it, but that doesn't make it less horrible.

I pull away from his embrace slowly. Slowly, because I know this is probably the last time our lips will touch, and even though I know now that he isn't the one, kissing him is still a very pleasant thing. There's just someone I'd rather be kissing instead.

'Haruki . . . ' I whisper in a pained voice. 'I'm sorry. I can't do this.'

He frowns again, like he did earlier, like he doesn't fully recognize me. Like he's trying to understand why. 'Wait. What? What's wrong?' He touches his thumb to his lips almost absentmindedly. 'Did you not want me to? Your answer was a little ambiguous.'

'No. Yes. I mean –'

A raised eyebrow. 'Do you see my issue?'

I laugh, but the guilt cuts through it and I stop. I force myself through this awful conversation. 'I mean I can't do this. Us.' A beat, as I figure out how much I should tell him.

'But I forgive you,' he says, and I hate the note of pleading in his voice. 'All of it, Caro. Yeah, the pills were kinda messed up, but what I feel for you –'

I have to tell him the full truth. I've come this far. So I swallow the lump in my throat, and say, 'I like someone else, and it's not fair on you.'

As I say the words aloud, I swear the external volume in the hallway is turned down to mute. There are hundreds of kids swarming around us, and it's like every single one of them stops talking at once. They don't, of course. It's just the sheer terror and guilt fucking with my eardrums. But still.

'Oh. Wow. Okay.' Haruki nods, even though it's at odds with what he's saying. 'That's . . . not what I was expecting.'

'Honestly, me neither.' I keep my voice low, so paranoid about being heard it's like I'm smoked a thousand joints all at once. 'I've liked you for so long. I've loved you, even. But this other . . . person? They've caught me off-guard. And I need to see what it is. What it could be.'

His dark eyes scan mine. They look dangerously shiny, but it could be the strip lighting. 'It's Keiko.'

280

'How did –'

'At the gig. I knew then, I think. I just didn't want to admit it.' He gestures at the brownie box. 'And like . . . she's not exactly subtle.'

I chuckle to try and dissipate some of the tension. 'You could've given me a heads-up, dude. It's taken me until now to figure out.'

'That you're bi?'

The word catches me out. It sounds ridiculous, but I hadn't thought of it in those terms. Maybe because my feelings for Keiko have shapeshifted so much in the last few months that they've been impossible to pin down to a set definition. Maybe because I only fully confirmed them about forty seconds ago.

What I do know is that I want to be with her. And I wanted to be with Haruki too. A girl and a guy. Bisexual.

It seems like too simple a word for how I feel about Keiko, or about Haruki, or about myself. But it's a start.

'I . . . guess so,' I say. 'I guess I'm bi.'

And then I smile. The cool thing about having gay dads is that I'm excited to tell them. Vati is always complaining about how basic the Straights are.

'Good for you, Caro,' Haruki says, and not in a patronizing way. 'You're more true to yourself than anyone else I know. I always did like that.' Then he hangs his head, as though the reality of the break-up just hit him, and starts to walk away.

With a hollow pang, I realize how much I'll miss hanging out with him, talking about science and HEMA and the milkshake hierarchy. I'll miss the feeling of being around him, being seen by him, being loved by him. But asking for friendship after I just dumped him seems hella selfish, and I need to honor his lines, so I swallow my own sadness and resign myself to a Haruki-less life once more.

'Haruki!' I call after him, because there's something else I need to make sure of.

He stops a few feet away from me. 'Yeah?'

I chew my lip. 'Don't tell people, okay?'

'Oh.' He seems surprised. 'I mean, sure. But it's not a big deal. I hope you know that.'

'It is and it isn't,' I say softly. 'I can't explain.'

Haruki smiles warmly, if still with dejection. 'Of course.'

23

Keiko is nowhere to be seen all day. She's not in the auditorium, or the soundproofed music booths she sometimes uses to rehearse over free periods. She's not in the cafeteria at lunchtime, nor in any of the classes she's supposed to have.

Because I'm just generally Like That, I enjoy speculating over where she could be instead in order to make myself miserable. Maybe she bunked off to spend the day with Marieke! Maybe they're having sex right this second!

I picture them frolicking at the beach, or hunting the mall for a new outfit for Keiko's gig tonight. She's playing at a bigger venue in the city, which her manager set up in order to raise her profile, and they're sending a photographer to take some actual professional shots of her performing. She outgrew the website Gabriela and I made for her reeeeal fast.

In any case, I feel a little lonely after my break-up with Haruki. Gabriela is hanging out with the cheer squad, and I don't want to ping off a message to the group chat about what happened. They probably knew it was coming anyway, since I've stopped taking the pills, and besides, I want to tell Keiko face to face that I'm all hers – if she wants me.

After a bit of a blah day without my favorite people, I arrive home to a snoozing Sirius – the height of luxury after being humped senseless for weeks on end – and heated voices in the kitchen. I hover just beyond the doorway, true to sneaky form.

'You went into my personal files? And sent my incomplete manuscript to a literary agent?' Dad's voice is quiet and cold, which is how you know he's absolutely furious. 'How could you do this? You have made me look a fool. The book is not ready. This is a betrayal of trust, Felix, and frankly –'

In a way so playful it's almost mocking, Vati says, 'Oh, Michael, stop playing the insulted sausage.'

'WOULD YOU PLEASE STOP TALKING NONSENSE FOR ONCE IN YOUR RIDICULOUS LIFE.' Yes, he actually talks like he's speaking in caps lock. It is quite the thing to behold.

Vati retorts, 'That is highly racist and xenophobic, and *frankly* I expect better from a published author.'

This takes the wind from Dad's caps-lock sails. Even quieter, he asks, 'A published author?'

'Yes, Michael, if you would let an innocent husband finish, you would know that this literary agent wants to sign you as a client, because they already have interest from three of the major non-fiction editors to whom they have mentioned the book. Two are preparing offers as we speak, just based on this proposal and sample alone. So you see –'

'Do you actually mean to say that this book might sell after all?' Dad's voice is choked with emotion.

Goosepimples chasing up and down my arms, I shiver and peer around the corner as Vati unfolds his arms. 'It certainly appears that way, you cynical, cynical man.'

And then Dad *screams*. Actually screams with joy like a small child. He and Vati immediately start leaping around the kitchen, hands flapping like excitable geese.

'Caro will have some money for college!'

'She will, Michael, it is true!'

'I'm going to be a published author!'

'Michael! You just used a contraction! Forget it, the book deal is cancelled, there is no way New York wants you now. Honestly, such feeble grasp of the English lang—'

For once in his ridiculous life, Vati actually shuts up. He kind of has to, since Dad has started smooching him with such force that he loses his footing and almost collapses into Sirius's disgusting bed.

Maybe I'll save the whole coming-out thing for another day.

Instead of ruining their moment, I tiptoe quietly upstairs.

It's not that I don't want to share their joy with them – it's just that I want Dad to have *two* euphoric moments. One right now, smooching his husband as his one-eyed cockapoo watches from the sidelines, and the other when he gets to sit me down and tell me he's going to be a published author. That I'll be able to wander into my favorite Barnes & Noble's science section and see Dr Michael Murphy's groundbreaking book staring back at me. I tear up at the thought, content in my decision to let them be.

Besides. I have a gig to get ready for.

Tonight's venue – an old warehouse come street market come pop-up theatre come whatever hell else the owner comes up with – is around four times the size of the intimate bar I last saw Keiko perform in, and the tickets are double the price. As soon as I walk in, my stomach cramps with nerves. Not for what I'm about to do, but for Keiko. I want her to kill it up there. And I believe she will. But still, the second-hand fear is *real*. There are so. Many. People.

I arrive late, for me, because I actually gave my outfit a little thought. Turns out I don't possess any clothes that could conceivably be thought fashionable, so I end up raiding Vati's slightly eccentric closet. I find a pink-and-green tropical print button-down with short sleeves, which is hideous but sort of in that purposefully hideous way. I think. I can never really tell. Then I take some old black skinny jeans and tear holes in them up and down the front in that Hipster Manner. Keiko loves a distressed denim.

It's not like I'm dressing for her, though. I'm just finally having a little fun with what I wear, now that I have the confidence not to give a fuck what other people think. I throw on Dad's old Casio wristwatch, some beat-up Birkenstocks I usually wear to 'garden' with Vati, and a half-dried-up purple lipstick Gabriela gifted me last Christmas.

When I check my reflection in the mirror by the front door, I grin. I look completely ridiculous, but completely Caro. Maybe this is the way *I* can have fun with clothes, by wearing second-hand stuff that's meaningful to me. Stuff that sums me up – a weird mix of pragmatism and eccentricity.

I don't even worry about whether Keiko will like it. She'll just be glad it's not a plain white tank top and jean shorts.

Anyway, because I'm not as early as usual, by the time I grab a Cherry Coke, Keiko's band have already taken the stage.

The taiko drums kick in, then the gongs and the flutes and the guitars, and the crowd is *really* feeling it. It's a different clientele tonight. Whereas the last gig was made up almost entirely of pre-existing Keiko fans, this audience seems more like a bunch of college students looking for somewhere new to get wasted and/or high. Which isn't necessarily a bad thing – it's a chance for her to win over a whole new set and build her fanbase full of people who'll be able to say 'I saw her back when.'

But there's a more frantic energy than before, and a lot of people on a lot of drugs, and I start to panic that I've done the wrong thing in coming. I told Dad and Vati it would be safe, and also a little white lie that I'd be backstage the whole time. Did I make the wrong call? What if I get caught up in something nasty here?

The second Keiko walks on stage, though, all of my worries disappear. The frenetic crowd melts into a haze.

She's absolutely slaying in a crisp white jumpsuit with cut-out sections around her waist, exposing strips of soft, pale brown skin. The postbox-red lipstick perfectly matches her enormous crimson platform shoes, and her lilac hair is coiffed into an elaborate fifties updo.

She is so beautiful.

As the taiko drums suddenly die down, the air is thick with anticipation. She leaves it for a perfect beat, then opens her mouth and launches straight into *Upside Downside*.

This time there are no fan-girl screams, but people are really into it. They dance wildly to the up-tempo beat, swinging warm beer around in the air, marching on the spot to the beat of the drums.

I push to the front right as Keiko finishes her opener and yells, 'Whaddup, Charleston? How are we doin' tonight?'

Lingering a few rows deep so she doesn't spot me too soon, I settle into the set, losing myself in the words and the melodies and the incredible composition. Keiko's confidence is astounding. She performs like every single last person in this room is already a convert, like she knows she's going to be the next Beyoncé and they're just lucky to witness her coming up.

And it works. Slowly but surely, almost everyone goes from dancing in a circle with their friends to turning to face Keiko, watching her own the stage. They're still dancing, but now they're really focused on what they're dancing to. *Who* they're dancing to.

Then comes the moment I came here for. The opening bars of *Bones and Stardust* kick in. And I move right to the front.

She doesn't see me yet. She just starts singing, eyes closed, feeling every word.

Why are you so afraid?
Why are you so afraid of your own reflection
When your reflection is the stars you love
The sky above
Is in you
Why are you so afraid when you are the universe
And the universe is you?

Why are you so afraid?
Why are you so afraid of your own dimensions
When your dimensions are your history
There's eternity
Within you
Why are you so afraid when you are the universe
And the universe is you?

Right before she launches into the chorus, she opens her eyes. And she sees me.

It does not go as planned.

'Fuck!' she whispers into the mic.

I grin so hard I have to bite down on my bottom lip to stop a laugh from escaping.

Keiko being Keiko, she styles the 'fuck' into the song, repeating the word until it goes from breathy and ethereal to passionate and fiery.

Fuck
Fuck
Fuck
You are bones and you are stardust
And you must, you must not betray
Your reflection, your dimensions
Not to mention

The love that burns inside you
Like bones and stardust

And honestly I'm not just saying this because it's my fault, but I really think the cursing adds something.

After she finishes the set, I push through the throngs of newly converted Keiko stans and find the entry to what I assume must be backstage. A burly bouncer holds out his forearm to prevent me going through.

I show him my own forearm, of the fresh tattoo inspired by *Bones and Stardust*. 'That song was about me, sir.'

He raises an intimidating eyebrow. 'Y'all know how many crazy fans get tattoos of their idol's lyrics?'

'No! Really. I'm Keiko's . . . best friend. Maybe more. That's actually why I'm here.'

I hold up my phone and show him the background of me, Keiko and Gabriela.

He barely looks. 'A'ight, I don't need the PBS special of y'all's drama. Talent!' he yells through the back. 'Yo, talent. Over here. There's someone to see you. Come check she's cool so a dude can smoke.'

He's barely finished the sentence before Keiko arrives breathlessly by his side and says, 'Yeah. Yeah, she's cool.'

Some strands of her updo have come loose, and the strap of her jumpsuit has slid down her shoulder. Her eyes are wild with adrenaline.

Wordlessly, I follow her down a corridor and into a semi-private corner of the backstage area, by a dressing table laden with eyeshadow palettes, hairspray, and half-finished bottles of water. She looks like she's about to flump down into the chair, but then decides against it and hovers awkwardly by the edge of the table instead. It's the first time I've ever seen her look a little nervous around me, and it does funny things to my insides.

Not knowing how to start, I say, 'You were amazing, Kiks.'

She smiles, but it's a little stiff. 'You never get tired of saying that?'

'You never get tired of being it?'

A sharp bark of laughter. 'Fuck no.'

'Then fuck no also.'

She shakes her head. 'I can't believe you made me swear on stage.'

'Yeah. Was it the shirt?'

She looks at it as though seeing it for the first time. 'It is . . . a lot. You know, visually. In a good way, though.'

'Thanks. It's Vati's.'

'That makes sense.'

There's an awkward pause. Another band starts up on stage, and they sound extremely dull compared to Keiko's whirlwind set.

Okay. Here goes.

'Listen. The reason I came here is because . . . I wanted to say all the things I should've said to you on the carousel. You know, before I nearly snapped my neck.'

She arranges the water bottles in a line. 'Honestly, Caro, we're cool. You don't have to –'

'Will you shut up and listen to me for once in your life?' I interrupt, for once in my life.

That gets her attention. She looks up at me, half-bemused, half-impressed. 'Alright.'

I had a whole spiel prepared. A whole spiel about how my feelings for her have changed and evolved, about how I think about her all the time, about how there's nobody else I would rather be around, nobody who makes me happier. A whole spiel about how nobody makes me like myself more. A whole spiel about how I want to kiss her, and only her. A whole spiel about how the way I feel about her is dark energy in action. All love is. And at some point, we just have to stop analyzing it, and trust that it will only continue to grow.

But all that comes out is this:

'I love you. I'm *in* love with you.'

She freezes in shock. A smile is playing around the corners of her red lips, but she holds it back, as though she won't let herself believe what she just heard. 'Wait. What?' I don't notice how badly her hands are shaking until I see her clasp them together.

'I'm in love with you, Keiko.' I'm surprised how calm and clear my voice is. 'I just wanted to be sure that the way I felt wasn't because of the pills. That the way *you* felt wasn't because of the pills. My heart couldn't take losing you like that. Now the pills are gone, and I know what I'm feeling is real. But I'm done trying to manipulate how other people feel about me. So I'm asking you, right now . . . how do you feel about me? Please know that any answer is okay. You could literally be like, I want to assassinate you with a longsword and I'd be like, I respect that.'

She bursts out laughing. 'You're such a nerd.'

'What on earth is nerdy about a longsword?' I ask sincerely.

'I love you too,' she breathes. 'I'm in love with you too.'

I soak in every inch of the moment; the alt-rock in the background, the scent of hairspray and jojoba, the lilac hair and red lips and the absolutely remarkable girl they belong to.

The girl who loves me like I love her.

The girl I finally feel like I'm good enough to be with.

'Can we kiss now?' I ask, and now I'm the one who's shaking, because Keiko has kissed many girls and I have kissed precisely none, and sure it's probably the same as kissing boys but also it's really, really not.

She responds by pushing off the dressing table and closing

the distance between us. For a few moments before our lips touch, she just lingers there, no more than an inch away, and it's so strange to have my best friend so close to me, so strange to *want* her like this.

When we finally kiss, it feels entirely different to any kiss I've ever had before. It's softer and deeper, and terrifying and life-affirming, like a piece of my heart is finally clicking into place. Like all the dark energy finally has a place to go.

Wait. Maybe this dark energy – the mysterious matter that caused my feelings for Keiko to expand – maybe it was self-love all along. Maybe it was the belief that I actually deserved someone like her.

There are a lot of maybes in that paragraph. If I pursue a career in astrophysics, and if I keep falling in love with Keiko in new and mysterious ways, there will be many more maybes to come.

And that's okay. That's fucking great, in fact. Because if there's anything I've realized in the last few months, it's that guarantees suck the fun out of life, and love, and everything in between.

I'm done chasing guarantees. And I'm done living like love is a science problem to be solved.

There's science involved, of course. There's science in everything. Estrogen and testosterone, adrenaline and dopamine and serotonin. Oxytocin and vasopressin. Sex pheromones. Dark energy.

But what I have learned is that some things *shouldn't* be put under a microscope and dissected. The more we analyze and unravel and reduce love, the more we break it, like we do to the universe every time we try too hard to understand it.

That's it. That's the Love Hypothesis.

It was right in front of me all along.

THE END

Acknowledgments

This is my sixth published book, and it'll never fail to amaze me just how much hard work — from so, so many people — goes into making the story in my head a real thing the world can read. An enormous shout out to everyone at Egmont for believing in me, and working so hard on this book: Liz Bankes (and her extraordinary editorial eye), Ali Dougal, Sarah Levison, Lucy Courtenay, Laura Bird, Hilary Bell and Siobhan McDermott. And to Lauren James, for offering editorial guidance on the sciencey bits!

As ever, a huge thank you to my incredible agent, Suzie Townsend, for her never-ending support, advice and hard work on my behalf. I say this in every acknowledgments section, but I wouldn't be doing this job if you hadn't taken a chance on 22-year-old me, and I'm so grateful. Also a massive thank you to everyone at New Leaf, particularly Pouya Shahbazian for fighting so hard to get this book to the screen, Maíra Roman, Veronica Grijalva, Dani Segelbaum and Mariah Chappell. What a dream team.

My writing pals! Seriously, what would I do without you? There are far, far too many to name and I'm grateful to all of you, but a special shout out to my agency siblings Francina Simone, Sasha Alsberg, Margot Wood, Victoria Aveyard, Claribel Ortega and Emma Theriault.

I'm just realizing how many people I'm listing are women. Who run the world? (Sorry, Pouya.)

Speaking of which, ten thousand thank yous to Helen Lederer and the Comedy Women In Print Prize judges for crowning *The Exact Opposite Of Okay* the inaugural winner. It came at a time when I so badly needed the boost, and it bolstered me to keep writing my funny, flawed characters.

Permanent shout out to my friends and family for putting up with my nonsense, including my dog Obi, whose beautiful furry head is currently resting very unhelpfully on my laptop keyboard. Mum, Dad, Jack, Gran, the rest of my bonkers family, Toria, Nic, Lucy, Hilary, Hannah, Lauren, Amy, Spike, Steve, Heather. Oh, and the Mslexia crew – thank you for welcoming me back with open(ish) arms.

And to Louis – my husband, best friend, soul mate, and by the time this book hits shelves, father to our tiny baby son. I love you both more than any hypothesis can explain.